# HIS STOLEN INNOCENT'S VOW

MARCELLA BELL

MILLS & BOON

First published in Great Britain 2021
by Mills & Boon, an imprint of HarperCollins*Publishers* Ltd,
1 London Bridge Street, London, SE1 9GF

www.harpercollins.co.uk

HarperCollins*Publishers*
1st Floor, Watermarque Building,
Ringsend Road, Dublin 4, Ireland

Large Print edition 2021

His Stolen Innocent's Vow © 2021 Marcella Bell

ISBN: 978-0-263-28877-3

07/21

**MIX**
Paper from
responsible sources
FSC
www.fsc.org   **FSC** C007454

To Kaleen, my real-life Hel.

# CHAPTER ONE

HELENE COSIMA D'TIERRZA, inheritor of the great d'Tierrza fortune and titles—including the duchy—and seventh in line for the throne of Cyrano, stood unsteadily before the marble statue that dominated her family's private courtyard.

Her silver-blond bangs feathered across her brow, swaying in time with her body's slight motion, while her normally sharp sapphire-blue eyes glared with unfocused intensity at the carved figure's face. Her dress was a long column of azure. Strapless and simple, it emphasized the elegant length of her figure rather than the unexpected muscle tone of her arms and chest. The dress flared gently at its base to provide what she supposed was a generous allowance for walking…if one minced.

Disgust curled her lips, the effect all the

more striking for the fullness of her wide mouth.

Today might be the one day of the year she conceded to wearing a dress, but she never minced.

It was also the one day of the year when she drank.

Both the dress and the drink contributed to the uncharacteristic wobble in her stance.

With her arms crossed in front of her chest and a half-empty flute of champagne loosely clasped in one hand, angled at a slight tilt, she was also uncharacteristically alone. She had no one to guard and no staff lingered in the shadows. They were occupied with the guests gathered in the large seascape courtyard who mingled and drank, all in the dubious name of her father's legacy.

The king and queen, two of her most constant companions, were in attendance, as was her fellow queen's guard, Jenna Moustafa, who was on solo duty with backup from the king's guard while Hel played dress-up.

The crease between her eyebrows deepened. She should be out there with her friends, alert and ready to back up Moustafa should the need arise. It would certainly be a better use of her time than standing in front of her father's likeness, once again engaged in the silent battle of wills that hadn't so much as ended with the end of his life, as become unwinnable. Not that she ever had a chance when he'd been alive. No one stood a chance against Dominic d'Tierrza.

Hel wouldn't be the one to throw in the towel, though. Her father didn't deserve the satisfaction.

Not even in death.

Instead, she sneered at the statue. "You've really outdone yourself this year, Papa. Already raised two million and we haven't even had dinner yet."

He said nothing in response.

He wouldn't have, had he been alive, either. Speaking about money was gauche and two million a paltry sum. He would have raised four by this point in the afternoon had he been around to run things. His permanently raised eyebrow said as much.

*Not up to the standard of the d'Tierrza name.*

Though just a memory, the oft-repeated words remained an acid refrain.

Her father had been old-fashioned, autocratic and hateful. She'd only learned the last in her teens. He cared about the family line and that alone.

A daughter was a bargaining chip to be played to the family's best advantage, nothing more. A wife past childbearing years, even less.

He had encouraged Helene, named after the beautiful cause of the Trojan War, to be lovely and amenable, a prize all men would covet.

So she had become loud and opinionated and learned to fight.

She'd also gone out into the world and gotten involved, gotten dirty, done everything she could to prove that Helene d'Tierrza was the furthest thing from the marriage material her father wanted her to be as was possible.

It hadn't been enough.

Nothing, not even truly diverging from her "correct" path to become a royal guard, had truly been enough to get back at him, to balance the scales. Not when he'd been alive and certainly not now that he was dead.

Not when he still cast such a long shadow over her life. Over her mother's.

She couldn't even believe they were doing an event in his name. There was nothing honorable about her father's legacy—it was only criminal.

She could literally recite a list of crimes.

But she never did, merely carried it around with her—a small penance for the ills he wrought on the world, and the only one she'd been allowed. On the point that the d'Tierrzas were important to national security, it seemed the world agreed with her father.

She and her mother kept their dirty laundry hidden in the dark and everyone benefitted. And maybe if she dedicated every living and breathing moment to serving justice, it might make up for the lie…if not the actual sins of her father.

Besides, the money they raised went to charities across the entire island nation.

That wouldn't have mattered to her father, though. Only the d'Tierrza name mattered to him. Nothing else. No other name, not even that of the royal family, could be allowed to outshine it.

God help you if you had the misfortune to be born with that name.

The charities mattered to her, though. People mattered to her. She was related to him in name only, and if she'd at first cultivated heart and honor just to spite him, in the end, those qualities had been too pure to pollute and had instead molded her. Including the voice that told her all of this was wrong.

Hel broke her stare, unfolded her arms and lazily downed the remainder of her champagne. Effervescent and smooth, it bubbled gently down her throat while she contemplated the perfect crystal stem twirling between her fingers. Then, without turning her gaze back to the statue, she stopped twirling the glass and flicked her wrist, the action decisive and controlled.

The glass sailed toward her father's likeness, spinning end over end in a perfect circle, before it crashed into the marble statue, shattering on impact. Bright clear pieces of crystal caught the light as they fell, filling the space with her own personal rainbow, all to the sound of tiny brittle stars cracking on the ground.

Suddenly, she heard a throat clear and the scuffing of feet on the paving stones behind her. In an instant, she snapped into full alertness, her wobble and dead father abandoned.

Behind her, the stranger quickened. She moved faster, feinting to the right and dropping into a crouch, before a large hand came around to catch her around the mouth. Her dress seam split as she executed the move, but she ignored it, spinning around to shoot her heeled foot out at the shin of her would-be abductor.

The person anticipated the move, though, jumping out of both her reach and sight. She tried to leap upright but lost precious time, slowed down as she was by her torn evening gown. Their arms, large and strong, came around hers, holding her tight in an iron grip.

This was exactly why she refused to wear dresses. She wouldn't have been caught if she'd had pants on.

She slammed her head back toward her attacker's face, but once again the stranger anticipated her move and shifted their head to the side in time to avoid her. Arms tightened around her. She lifted her feet, surprising them with her entire body weight. There was a grunt behind her, but the person held on, the powerful grip loosening only a fraction.

The fraction was all she needed.

She twisted down and out of the hold, dropping to the ground at the same time as she swept his feet out from under him. She could see that he was a man now. He landed well, but the move managed to give her enough time to put space between them and take a reasonable, if narrow, fighting stance.

He leaped from the ground effortlessly and advanced toward her, and for an instant, she was frozen.

He was stunning.

Well over six feet tall, his skin shone a rich, dark brown. His suit was impeccably tailored but not of Cyranese cut or style. Instead, it nodded toward their Sidran neighbors to the south with a long jacket and short collar.

In all her life, she had never been stopped short by another soul, and yet this man had paralyzed her. It wasn't his clothing, though it fit him flawlessly, highlighting his perfect proportions. The bulk of the people who inhabited her world had been wearing bespoke couture since they could first toddle. It wasn't his height. Her father had been a tall man and her cousin, the current king and her lifelong best friend, was a towering man.

The man was older than she was, his trim beard lightly salt and peppered, though his skin was as smooth as marble. His eyebrows were thick and black, and low over his eyes.

Those eyes. Something about them grabbed at her and pulled, urging her to move closer, as if she was his prey, helplessly ensnared.

He smiled, the expression filling his deep brown eyes with an arrogant gleam. The smile drew her eyes to his mouth, which was full. Her lips parted, dry suddenly, and she licked them.

"It seems I might have underestimated the difficulty I'd face in convincing you today…"

he mused in Cyranese, his low whisper a skin-tingling bass that caressed her ears.

She shivered, breath hitching, as her body kick-started systems she'd been certain were defective after years of being dormant.

And then his words sank in.

He knew the effect he was having on her. And he thought he could use it against her.

Heat flooded Hel's face, a combination of irritation at his arrogance and embarrassment at her stupefaction—because that's the only thing it could be called, as stupid as it was—but this time she didn't let her reaction to him slow her down.

In one smooth motion, she reached down, took off a heel and hurled it at his face, quickly repeating the motion with the other shoe before bolting toward the courtyard's exit.

He avoided the first shoe, but not the second, giving her precious seconds of advantage.

They weren't enough.

Beating her to the archway, he blocked the way and she halted, not willing to get within arm's reach again. Without taking her eyes off him, she grabbed the ripped seam of her dress and ripped it farther.

His cocky grin returned. "Eager, are we?"

She flipped him a rude gesture and he threw his head back and laughed. The sound hummed through her bones before coming to a heated rest at her core, though she resisted the urge to press her legs together.

"Who are you?" she asked.

"Not who you expected to meet here?" he asked with mock surprise, the laughter in his voice setting off inner fires she didn't know could burn.

The heat from her core made its way up her neck to merge with the bright blush spots on her cheeks until her normally cool, pale skin burned a bright red across her entire body.

"This is a private courtyard."

He nodded. "I know."

"What are you here for?"

He tilted his head in a chiding fashion that somehow reminded her of her mother, as if he knew she could do better. "To speak with you. Isn't it rather obvious?"

"Normally, people who wish to speak with me approach from the front," she observed.

He shrugged, the movement fluttering his jacket. "It wouldn't be the first time I've come at things from a different angle."

She laughed, unable to help herself in the face of his blasé attitude. "What did you want to talk about?"

A wicked spark came to his eyes as he took in her partially exposed body, beginning at her bare feet and traveling slowly up, lingering at her breasts, before his gaze locked on hers.

She felt the look like a caress, making her breathing go short and heavy.

"Many things—reunions, new unions…" he said, the words trailing off slow like honey.

"We've never met." She spoke casually as she shifted her weight to the balls of her feet.

Something like pain flashed across his eyes, but was gone by the time his words came out, his voice entirely nonchalant as he said, "The two of us? No. But we've known each other our whole lives."

His words were intriguing, a siren mystery tempting her to ponder his meaning instead of thinking through her next move, but she wasn't going to bite. She couldn't afford the time it would take. She'd only requested one day off, no matter how fascinating the stranger who dangled the lure.

With shocking speed, she pivoted on her heel and erupted into a sprint, wincing as she dashed barefoot through the shards of broken champagne glass along the way.

And it was her own fault. Her father always said her rashness would come home to roost.

Her would-be kidnapper was on her tail alarmingly quickly, but she had the advantages of a head start and greater familiarity with the terrain.

Running right at the statue, she leaped, her feet planting squarely on her father's nose with an ominous crack as she used it to spring onto the tiled rooftop surrounding the courtyard. She landed hard, sliding slightly as she dislodged the tiles, sending some falling to crack on the marbled floor below.

Once she caught her balance, she scrambled toward the top bar of the roofs—the only place where running was actually feasible.

A loud thud behind her and a quick glance over her shoulder confirmed that her pursuer had not yet given up. That was fine. She hadn't, either.

She ran across the roof, her bare feet finding easy purchase on the familiar old wood. She followed the same route she and her cousin had taken as young daredevils looking for a bit of fun and a chance to terrify their tutors.

With any luck, the old trick would work on the man behind her, because his long strides were rapidly closing the space between them.

In the distance, she could hear the tasteful music and muffled chatter of the party. There was still time to veer right and head in that direction. Moustafa and the king's guard wouldn't hesitate to provide backup. However, there was a chance that the man was actually coming after her in an effort to get near to the king and queen. In which case, protecting them meant keeping him away. Besides, she could just imagine the horror on her mother's face when her daughter literally dropped into the middle of her party wearing nothing but a tattered evening gown.

But then again, maybe her mother wouldn't mind. The party would certainly be talked about long afterward.

She had promised her mother that she would settle down, though, and—her profession notwithstanding—for the most part, she had.

After her father's death, the need to tarnish the family name had lost its sense of urgency.

Her mother, her companion in the trenches, understood her motivation for upsetting the family wheelhouse and cared little for what gossip surrounded her daughter. Their relationship was close and open and far too strong to be shaken by rumor. But her behavior could still impact the way her mother was treated in society, whom she was allowed to see, what services she could solicit. Hel knew her mother would say it saved her from frequenting with fools, but hearing that her mother had been denied an appointment at her salon after Helene joined the royal guard had triggered the protective response that years of living with her father had developed in her. She wouldn't do anything that might limit her mother's hard-earned freedom.

So rather than seek backup, Hel stayed her course, nearly to the spot that she and her cousin had named The Leap of Death.

They'd discovered it when they were eleven, once again illicitly exploring the ducal palace's roof.

"If you jump from here you would land in the deep pool," Zayn had said with a frown on his face, the one young Helene recognized as his figuring face. She'd looked, gauged the necessary arch, then given him a wide grin. He'd shaken his head. She'd taken a running start and jumped.

He'd been right. Thankfully.

After that, The Leap of Death had become the preferred method of testing the mettle of each and every educator and mentor assigned to bring them to heel. With the exception of one, none had realized the jump was safe until their charges returned hours later.

Hel was banking on the phenomenon that watching her leap to her death at sea would have the same demoralizing effect on the man chasing her as it had on so many of her would-be educators.

Meanwhile, she could swim into the natural caves, then take the path back up to the palace and figure out who in the hell the guy was. And she could do it with pants on.

She made the final turn on the roof, a sharp left that angled her toward the sunrise balconies—it was the turn that would lead her to the leap.

The man remained close on her heels.

Abruptly, she sprang off the beam, her body arching into a perfect dive, her blood singing a thrilling song she hadn't heard in too long.

Blood rushed in her ears as she angled toward the water, her body lighting to the experience like a long-lost friend.

Laughter bubbled out of her underwater.

She needed to do this more often.

She'd entered the water as slick as a seal, her momentum taking her another thirty yards before she surfaced.

Breathing heavily, she looked up at the corner of the roof she had jumped from, taken, as always, by how small and far away it looked. Her pursuer was nowhere to be seen. A wide grin spread across her face. The Leap of Death had come through once again.

She set a leisurely pace swimming back toward the caves, entering their shadowed depths quietly, her feet appreciating the cool and cleansing sting of the salt water after running through the broken glass.

And then she heard the sound of something large landing in the water.

Spinning around, she treaded water as she squinted in the direction of the sound. For a moment, all she saw was gently waving sea.

Then he surfaced.

She turned back to the cave, swimming furiously now, but he cut through the water behind her like some kind of sinister merman.

As she pushed deeper into the cave, a large shape took form, and she stopped in her swim. Once again treading water, her gasp was magnified and echoed by the curvature of the cave's walls.

There was a ship anchored in the cave.

Masculine laughter broke out behind her,

swirling around her, surrounding her in the high-ceilinged space.

Mere feet separated them in the water. She considered her next move. There was no way she could outswim him. She sensed it without a doubt, not needing to test the hypothesis.

There was something about him, his aura somehow half sea creature. Or maybe it was the fact that he seemed completely at one with the water, despite the fact that he swam in soaking-wet formal wear.

Of course, even against impossible odds, it never hurt to try.

Darting away from him, she put all her energy into speed and zoomed with a mad burst through the water.

And it worked. Shooting yards ahead of him, she felt the exhilaration of defeating a worthy opponent. It was certainly a better way to spend her father's birthday than pretending to love and honor him.

At that moment, the strength of her surge circled back to bite her. Swimming with enough speed to retain her lead required her

full power, all of her energy driving ahead…
straight into a tangle of net.

Caught in thoughts and swimming through
churning waters, she'd missed it, floating in
the water ahead of her.

Her momentum sent her into the net in a
tangle of limbs before the heavy waterlogged
ropes, now knotted around, began to drag her
below the surface. She struggled, but only
tangled herself further.

He was on her in seconds, securing her
around the waist with the iron band of his
arm. He was treading water while untangling
the ropes from her limbs with the other arm.

The water was his ally, accepting him as
one of its own while he worked smoothly, as
if they weren't bobbing in a cove.

Smoothly, until the palace alarm sounded
above them.

Her absence had been noted.

Cursing under his breath, he made quick
work of the last of the grasping ropes before pulling them with fast strokes toward
the ship.

"None of this is going according to my plan." He sounded like a weary grandfather.

She ignored him, aiming for a casual tone, though it was strained. "At least this answers how you got in."

The whole experience was turning out to be enough to throw her off balance. It wasn't every day a handsome stranger snuck his ship into her harbor and beat her at sparring. She was usually the one who won.

"I assume that's your ship?" she asked, as if the answer was of no importance.

He laughed, the sound once again echoing in the chamber of the cave, but said nothing.

They were nearly to the hanging rope ladder that would carry them onto the ship. She was exhausted, with welts beginning to form on her skin from her bout with the fishing net, and she blamed it on the dress.

If she hadn't been wearing a dress, they wouldn't have even made it to the harbor. She would have easily subdued the mesmerizing man in the family courtyard, learned what he wanted and ended the day nestled snugly in her childhood bed. It was becoming clearer and clearer to her that he had never intended to kidnap her, and that, as he carried them up the ladder with a slight huff to his breath and a new, more serious intensity now that the alarm had sounded, it might have actually made things more inconvenient for him.

Pondering all of this meant she didn't fight as he scaled the rope ladder with one arm and climbed aboard, his other arm holding her all the while.

Men and women of assorted shapes and sizes milled about on the deck, but no one seemed to bat an eye as he carried Hel aboard. A few even paused in what they were doing to wave and nod in greeting.

He acknowledged them with the briefest nod en route to wherever they were going.

The cabin he took her into was like walking into a Moroccan library—bright, airy and warm, with blindingly white walls lined with sleek bookshelves made from a honey-colored wood and large-sized porticos and skylights that drenched the room with sunbeams. It was utterly masculine, with its streamlined, low-profile decor, with soft, low-profile furniture, and each and every surface bare and clean enough to eat from. Each bookshelf was quite full and had a small lip. The lip, she presumed, was to keep the books where they were meant to be in the event of turbulent seas. The immense collection, she presumed, was for show, though the tradition was to pretend otherwise. In her lifetime, Hel had observed that men of action were rarely readers. Readers spent their evenings at home, not out at sea.

Yet, looking closer, she noticed signs of wear and tear—and not light—marking each volume: cracked spines, slightly bent covers, warped lines.

His books had not just been read. They'd been loved soft.

Despite the utter maleness of the room, no one would have called the space sterile or aggressive. Instead, it was warm and natural. Rich, vibrant-hued upholstery—goldenrod-yellow suede leather for the accent chair and deep burgundy silk for the matching sofa—and the woven wool throw pillows made the room homey. At their feet was a handwoven rug in a black-and-white Berber style on gleaming hardwood whose honey tones matched the bookshelves. Centered on the rug was a large, single-slab driftwood table, three inches thick and gleaming in the room's natural lighting, unabashedly gorgeous in all its Technicolor wood-grain glory.

So unless she was mistaken and this was *not* the wealthiest vessel she'd ever stumbled upon, the absolute lap of luxury, boasting subtle features here and there that even an aristocrat like herself might have trouble getting her hands on, this man was not hurting for cash.

Beneath the room's warmth, however, were signs she was dealing with a professional.

Surveillance cameras whispered in the corners of the room and there were items cleverly designed to look like pieces of the room that she was certain were weapons—a bookend, the unique detachable legs of a globe stand and an evil eye that hung on a long slender cord that she would have called a garret, if it hadn't been attached to one of the few pieces of decor in the cabin. There was a safe camouflaged among the books. It was one of the best jobs Hel had ever seen.

The man had money, a ship and he was paranoid. Putting the three things together, she could come to just one conclusion.

He was a pirate.

Hel had been kidnapped by pirates.

But why would a pirate kidnap her? Tierrza, her estate, was a port, but she didn't have any problems with pirates. They'd never truly had pirates, just smugglers, and her ancestors had dealt with them long ago.

But modern pirates still plagued the Mediterranean.

Just not usually Cyrano.

Hel quirked her lips, the private joke sliding across her mind that it was a sign her cousin, King Zayn, was succeeding in putting their island nation on the map. The fact that she was once again the one making jokes, even if just privately and in her mind, felt like a sign she'd only momentarily lost her groove—a brief blip in what was otherwise a perfect record.

Well, no one would really ever call her record perfect, but she was a damn good guard.

"Are you done with your tour? Forgive me if not, it just seemed like you had moved on." His voice was dry, filled with a joke just for him, leaving Hel with the strangest sense of being left out…and caring about it.

Hel's eyes narrowed, but she was determined to meet him head-on, even if she was barely clothed. "It's all right, some nice stuff in here, but it's just one room." She paused and looked around again, exaggerating the whole thing, then added with a disappointed frown, "And it's kind of small."

He let out a bark of laughter and she started, the sound entrancing her momentarily, a real-life version of the Pied Piper's flute. "Size doesn't matter, it's the motion of the ocean." His eyes laughed as he delivered the line with no shame, his open palm gesturing at the open sea around them through the porticos.

Hel forced herself to look away, following the path of his hand to stare hard at the water and grumbled, "That's not the ocean."

She didn't know what was wrong with her,

but it was certainly not helping her regain her accustomed advantage. It was hard to maintain discomfiting nonchalance, the strategy that seemed to most put her opponents off balance, when her breath kept catching every time her eyes snagged on this man's form, carrying her away with reactions and…staring, rather than cool observation.

Thinking while she could, while the strange distraction of him was out of sight, she reviewed what else she knew. Based on the level of luxury of the cabin, the obvious wealth it required to create such a space, let alone what might lie behind the two doors in the room, indicated this was the cabin's quarters. She could be wrong, of course, but she doubted it. She didn't know many people with the kind of wealth that could outfit a passenger or crew cabin so well. Very few were *that* rich, and she knew most of them.

Pirates were a rare thing in this day and age—in the Mediterranean or elsewhere, for that matter.

Incredibly wealthy pirates even less so.

In fact, there was only one who fit the bill

that she knew of, and it was, fortunately to the present context, her job to know things, but he wasn't a pirate. He was a privateer, and his name wasn't whispered with fear, but called out for in desperation.

Hel's stomach fluttered and it dawned on her that this is what people meant when they said they had butterflies, but she turned back to face him. Caught all over again by his arresting beauty, it took her a moment to speak, but when she did, despite the strength and steadiness of her voice, the strange absurdity of her words was enough to almost turn them into a question. Because in no scenario in all of the world did it make sense for a man famous through the entire Mediterranean for fighting human trafficking to be kidnapping her, she thought, as she said, "You're the Sea Wolf."

# CHAPTER TWO

EYEING HIS CAPTIVE, with her long, deadly limbs, her mop of silver-blond hair, her flashing gemstone eyes and skin that gave off a faint radiance—as if moonglow emanated from her very core, or she was a pearl come to life—Drake Andros, retired admiral, occasional investor, eternal sailor, licensed privateer and Sidran duke, held back a laugh.

"Caught me," he said with a smile instead.

That she'd put the pieces of his high-seas identity together was as irrelevant as it was charming, but he hadn't expected it of her. Not that he had been operating under the impression that she was stupid. Certainly not. A stupid woman didn't graduate at the top of her class from a military academy and rise through the ranks of the royal guard while successfully managing multiple complex estates. He was simply surprised that she'd maintained such an incredible level of cool-headed composure through the process of being accidentally kidnapped and literally dragged out to sea.

A phenomenal bout, superb high dive and hundred-meter swim, all wrapped it up with her being carried off, and she still had the wherewithal to come to an accurate conclusion with very little input—it was impressive. He could recognize that being impressed was sexist—he wouldn't be of a man in her position—but his inner demons were as irrelevant to the situation as was her lovely mind.

That he was the Sea Wolf was business. What sat between them was entirely personal.

Thirty years ago her father had tried to murder his family.

Today he'd achieved his vengeance.

But his plan hinged on her cooperation.

"So why did the Sea Wolf capture the Cyranese captain of the queen's guard?" she asked, adorably nonchalant about the whole thing.

"The Sea Wolf," he said, "doesn't have anything to do with you. Drake Andros, son of

Ibrahim and Amira Andros, rightful heir to the Andros Duchy of Cyrano, however, has a few things he'd like to discuss."

She froze, her face losing its pretty glow, replaced by a more deathly pallor.

Her reaction was…interesting. He had expected to have to feed her a few more tidbits before she began to realize the more sinister nature to their connection. Perhaps she wasn't unaware of what her father had done to him?

If that was true, it would change things. His gut tightened. He worked hard to account for contingencies, but by their nature, not every one could be anticipated. The tightness tilted toward a slow burn as his mind played out the ways his plan would be impacted if she wasn't as innocent as he'd assumed. Her original involvement would have been impossible—she'd been a small child—but had she a part in keeping the event covered up?

After all the years, all the loss…could he let it crumble if touching her was unconscionable? He hadn't had a problem touching her to this point. If she was guilty in the whole thing, as well, what did that say about the trust he could place in his own instincts where she was concerned?

As seconds passed, her reaction only seemed to deepen, actual horror dawning on her face just before she began to shake her head.

The suspicion that had started sick and slick and warm in his gut turned hot and dangerous as it unfurled.

She might not have been involved in the original plot, but her reaction suggested she wasn't innocent of it.

Emotion made him impatient, edgy. Life had consistently proved to him that the only thing he could rely on was himself, but what if even that wasn't true? What if he'd misread such a critical piece in her presumed innocence? If he'd been wrong he'd wasted years on a plot with a critical flaw. He'd done what his mother had warned him of and drilled so deep into the dark that he'd lost the light of clarity.

"Ibrahim Andros, your father's dearest friend and oldest childhood playmate, and his companion well into adulthood. They were two peas in one pod—right up until

Ibrahim, his wife, Amira, their son, Drake, and their daughter, Nya, all of them at once, were killed when their boat tragically capsized at sea."

Doubt turned his voice harsh and made his words run fast. His gaze was ultra penetrating as he watched her for hints or clues of guilt as he spoke, but if she already knew, then he wanted to be sure she felt at least something in his reveal—that she was moved, somehow, as she came to understand just exactly who he was, and what her family had made him.

"In the wake of the tragedy, your father became steward, and for all intents and purposes, inheritor of the slightly smaller duchy to the east, with its incredible maritime prospects, named as such, to the surprise of no one, by his very best friend."

"My father arranged the accident..." Her words were a breathless combination of horror, rage and knowing, all braided together.

But the knowing was a new knowing, and with taking it on, it seemed, she took on an invisible anchor of responsibility, her shoulders visibly sinking, though she had been barely old enough for school when it had all occurred.

Out of the storm of his emotions, he made the wild swing from suspicion to—to what exactly, he couldn't say, but something filled him with the urge to reach out to her, to place a hand on her shoulder and say something conciliatory, to remind her that she had been too young to have been meaningfully involved in the ancient plot.

He resisted the urge. Comforting her because her father was a monster was not on the current agenda. Wrenching his plan back on track and toward fruition was.

Though off to a less-than-smooth start, and thirty years delayed, justice would finally be served. His relief was shaky at best, the bumps and hurdles thus far only proving what he'd known since he was a disillusioned child: a person could only rely on themselves. That his plan hinged on her, a stranger and the daughter of his enemy, was a weakness, but one that could be adjusted to.

She was crucial to it all, the only one who could help him find the closure that he'd chased his whole life—closure that his mother had insisted had to come from within, not knowing that he didn't have anything inside but a gaping hunger for the wrongs committed against them to be righted—and already his plans had taken a significant detour because of it.

He had intended to approach her privately, smoothly lay his cards on the table based on his suspicion that she was of a mind with him, charm her into thinking she might be interested in destroying her father's legacy and leave the harbor with her none the wiser. He'd contemplated how to approach her for months, with the loft of their titles, the respective careers they were well known for in the world and the friendliness of their nations all on the line. Discretion, charm and mystery had been the key components of his planned approach.

Instead, they'd fought and set off a national alarm, and he'd unintentionally abducted her. And now he had to convince her to go along with his plan.

It was incredibly trying to work with others. He was cut from the cloth to lead or go alone—teamwork was inefficient.

But he could find no other way. Her father had been meticulous in his lineage obsession, ensuring that only another one of his blood, another d'Tierrza, could undo his work.

And so Drake had studied his would-be partner, reading every tabloid article about her and tracking down every whisper of her name from the moment his plans had settled into their final shape. He'd held his mother's hand as she struggled with her last breaths—cancer the foe that finally took her down after murder plots and poverty had tried their best and failed.

Before that moment, he had simply turned his entire life into a catalog of triumph and success, his metaphorical rude gesture to spite the man who'd tried to stamp out him and his family. But when he'd learned that that man had died, peacefully in his sleep, the death of the innocent and the just, while his mother had struggled to draw in air, it didn't matter that he'd made sure she'd had the best care money could provide and the all the comfort human beings had been able to invent. Drake had been consumed with impotent rage. That a good and strong woman would go, her passing a thing of pain, while her tormentor had gone easy ate at him, driving him from sleep, from home, from ease, from even the satisfaction of having earned everything back that had been taken from him and then some.

It wasn't enough. The only thing that could possibly be enough was to take everything that man held dear.

When the shocking announcement was made that the old duke had passed up his wife to name his daughter his successor, Drake realized he'd been given his opportunity.

Whether or not the father could see it, the daughter hated his guts.

Marrying her would be Drake's means to not just regaining his own ancestral home, but to taking Tierrza's, as well. He would exact his revenge in the only way that a man like Dominic d'Tierrza would have understood: by taking everything he had.

Helene might be the daughter of his greatest enemy, but she was also the key to his revenge. He was going to marry her. He was going to marry her and get her pregnant, and his sons—and his name—were going to rule not just Andros, but Tierrza, as well, the famous jewel of Cyrano.

And he had strong reason and evidence to believe that she would be amenable to the idea...if he hadn't irritated her too much by kidnapping and towering over her.

He didn't expect, however, her to place a hand over her heart as she said, "You have my most sincere apologies. If this world were a just one, my father would reap the punishment his actions deserved, but it is not, and this is just one more of the many evils he died without accounting for. I cannot undo what he did, but I offer you my deepest apologies." She concluded her speech with a deep bow.

He frowned.

This was not the solidarity he had been looking for.

He needed a rebellious daughter, not a battle-weary soldier.

Though, he supposed, her response was a

sort of confirmation of his suspicion that bad blood existed between father and daughter.

From age eleven to sixteen, she had used every public appearance and every form of acting out possible to present a clear picture, at least to Drake, of exactly what she thought of the man.

She had exhausted the typical means of wealthy children by the age of thirteen—wrecking cars, being caught on film smoking, dating older men. It had seemed her actions were more than adolescent rebellions. But then she'd turned to more mature methods.

At thirteen, she became famous for being the youngest accepted applicant for Cyrano's International Young People's Volunteer Corps, a humanitarian organization comprised of Cyranese citizens aged eighteen to twenty-six, sparking a sea of rumors of corruption and buying access that were no doubt true, but didn't prevent her from spending two years in Kazakhstan, mastering the Russian language and establishing an orphanage…into which she funneled an inordinate amount of d'Tierrza cash. The amount itself was the next scandal, far exceeding the highest recorded charitable donations in the nation of Cyrano prior to it. For a while, the joke was that daddy's little girl had a great big heart and no sense of the value of money. Again, it was clear to Drake, though, that she'd been entirely aware of her actions, and they were intentional.

She was hitting her father strategically.

Looking at her now, though, he realized it went deeper than that.

She wasn't merely a spoiled girl pushing back against her powerful father.

She was engaged in an honor war.

Helene d'Tierrza hated her father, and she had always taken pains to strike where she could to do the most damage—his pocketbook and his reputation.

The age of sixteen had brought an end to her obviously rebellious days, and by the end the year, marked a lull in her scandalous behavior. That birthday, Dominic d'Tierrza had announced her engagement to a Cyranese lord, the son of a known crony of her father's.

Three months later, the engagement was

over under murky circumstances. The young man left the country. Then, just before she turned seventeen, Helene shocked the world with her greatest scandal yet: enrolling in the Cyranese military academy. She kept a low profile for the remainder of her time in the academy, where she graduated six years later at the top of her class with top honors, as well as a master's degree in military sciences, making the society pages only for her academy honors.

She shocked Cyrano once more, however, upon graduation. Rather than return to her place in society, she enlisted in and was accepted as a member of the royal guard. That the female heir to the wealthiest aristocratic family in the country would postpone marriage in favor of active military duty was outrageous.

But by twenty-two it was clear that the Rebel Heiress, as she'd been dubbed by the tabloids, had settled into who she was. She'd been assigned to guard the then prince, Zayn, her cousin through her mother's family, and when his father was assassinated eleven years later, she found herself the guard of a king. Six months after that, upon the death of her father, she nonetheless became the Duchess d'Tierrza, the first female to hold the title in the history of the line. In fact, because there had never been a female head of the family, it had become a colloquial joke to refer to her as the duke.

This was all public knowledge. What Drake had pieced together from his own research, however, was that even after her father died, she continued to attack his legacy.

Rather than growing the d'Tierrza coffers, she managed her estates to perfection, bringing in greater incomes than they ever had under her father's watch, and donated all but what was required to manage each to charities around the nation. On the surface, it appeared she was increasing her family's income, but if one looked closely—as Drake had—she was incrementally shrinking the d'Tierrza estate and fortune, funneling wealth back into the community, little by little, through the charitable foundation she and her mother had created in her father's name.

And if he'd been left with any doubt before he approached her, she'd ended it by throwing a custom champagne flute at his likeness.

As Drake had suspected, her father's death didn't seem to have eased any of his daughter's animosity toward him, and for that, Drake was grateful, as his vengeance hinged on it.

"I'm sorry." She met his eyes—hers as blue as the deepest ocean—commander to commander, and he knew that her words weren't empty. He appreciated them, he truly did. But he needed a lot more than an apology from her.

But she wasn't done yet.

Wrapping her arms around her chest, a gesture that returned his attention to the fact that while she wasn't naked, she was also not what anyone would reliably describe as fully clothed, she said, "My father was a real bastard."

The reminder of her state of undress brought with it an unwelcome tightening in his groin, even as discussing her father left a sour taste in his mouth, so he was sharper than he intended to be when he said, "Take one of my shirts," then nodded toward the door closest to her, which led to his bedroom.

Without commenting on his sudden change of subject, she walked in the direction he indicated and returned with a shirt from his wardrobe.

She had selected quickly, choosing a navy blue button-up. She turned her back to him before she put it on. The back of her blue dress revealed bare shoulders and what remained of it after their chase hugged the long line of her spine before ending at midthigh, where jagged edges revealed the supple skin of her lower derriere as she put her arms in the sleeves… Then his shirt dropped down to cover it all up and for a split second he hated the garment.

When she turned around, however, he decided he loved it once more—would perhaps even call it his favorite shirt.

The dark blue fabric, which should have made her look washed out, only served to deepen the flashing blue of her eyes and make her white-blond hair shine like silver.

She was truly a stunning creature, what he imagined a Valkyrie might look like, cross-bred with a literal star.

Her eyebrows were deep golden blond, highlighting the elegant bone structure of her face. Her lips were sinful—bright coral, lush and carnal. They were a stark contrast to the rest of her untouchable cool beauty. And her nose was long and straight—aristocratic to the bone.

And all of that, coupled with her obvious hatred of her father, meant that when it came to this particular path to revenge, he might even enjoy the journey. Even if it did involve marrying and making love to the daughter of his greatest enemy.

"As you were saying…your father was a real bastard, which brings us to what I was hoping to speak with you about."

She nodded with a half smile, sitting on the arm of his chair as she did so, and his skin heated, his entire system thrilling as he circled ever closer to the achievement of his goals.

"I have a proposal for you, a way for you

to 'right the wrongs,' as you say. What I'm asking for is no small commitment, I recognize that, but the wrong your father committed against my family is no small thing, either. What I am asking for requires a two- or possibly three-year sacrifice from you and a great deal of physical discomfort, but afterward, you will be free to go your own, returning entirely to your life as it is now."

Crossing her arms in from her chest, she lifted an eyebrow. "A great deal of physical discomfort, eh? You're not selling this well."

Drake laughed, the sound starting as a low rumble in his gut and rising out of his reach and deep until his eyes watered. Wiping them at the corners, he shook his head. "Oh, it's nothing that women don't go through all over the world every day—I just want you to be the mother of my children."

# CHAPTER THREE

HEL'S MOUTH DROPPED OPEN.

It made her look like a fish. Roz, her childhood etiquette tutor and lifelong ally, had drilled this into her. She knew it like she knew her name, and yet there she was.

The man before her certainly kept her on her toes, that was for sure. He threw her off balance with an ease that no one but her father had ever been able to achieve.

He was gorgeous and tragic and dangerous and everything the angry daughter of a wealthy man could ask for when it came to flipping her father and family legacy the bird—everything she might have conjured up for herself, late at night in her room as a young girl, as yet powerless to stand up to her autocratic parent.

But she wasn't that girl anymore, and while

this thrilling man and his thrilling and indecent proposal were a temptation the likes of which her thrill-seeking heart might have leaped at earlier in her life, she had grown into the kind of woman that realized her responsibilities were more important than her desires. And if she was tempted in a way a part of her was ashamed of, she could at least find comfort in the truth of that fact, because she certainly wasn't finding it in the words she had to say.

"I can't," she said, though her mouth fought the words the whole time.

He smiled, and the smile was as entrancing as her first look at him had been. She had never had this reaction to another human. Yes, she had been wild and reckless in her youth, but it had all been for show. She hadn't been attracted to anyone she'd made sure to be photographed with, just like she'd never actually gone out with any of them. Though the scandal had suited her narrative, the reality had been the obvious truth: she had been too young for that kind of thing.

Later, in the Volunteer Corps and later in

the military academy, she had been too busy for it. And then she had been a royal guard and her job made it too risky. Then her father had died and her vow had put an end to even thinking about it. Until this shockingly magnetic man had dropped into her world out of the sky and brought desire to the forefront after it was far too late to do anything about it.

For the first time since she'd made it, she regretted her vow. Not the actual making of it—that she stood by—and not because she wanted to take it back, but because she'd had no idea what she'd been giving up when she had. Promises made in ignorance required keeping no less than those made in full knowledge, but if she'd known men like him existed in the world…

His voice was its own lure, warm like an embrace, confident in its assuredness that it could change her mind. "Of course you can't. It isn't done. You don't know me. What would people think…? But ignore that, ignore them. Think instead of what your father would think. Think about how angr—"

As much as she loved to imagine her father angry, she held up her hand to stop him where he was. "I can't," she repeated, her voice low and earnest. "I can't, because when I went to him as he lay dying, I looked him in his eye and swore to him that the d'Tierrza line would end with me, that there would be no d'Tierrza children to inherit the lands or title and that I would see to it that the family name was wiped from the face of the earth so that everything he had ever worked for, or cared about, was lost to history, the legacy he cared so much about nothing but dust. I swore to him that I would never marry and never have children, that not a trace of his legacy would be left on this planet."

For a moment, there was a pause, as if the room itself had sucked in a hiss of irritation. The muscles in his neck tensed, then flexed, though he remained otherwise motionless. He blinked as if in slow motion, the movement a sigh, carrying something much deeper than frustration, though no sound came out. Hel's chest squeezed as she merely observed him. She felt like she'd let him down in some monumental way though they'd only just become reacquainted. She struggled to understand why the sensation was so familiar until she recognized the experience of being in the presence of her father.

Then he opened his eyes again, and instead of the cold green disdain her heart expected, they still burned that fascinating warm brown—a heat that was a steady home fire, as comforting as the imaginary family she'd dreamed up as a child—and all of the taut disappointment in the air was gone.

Her vow was a hiccup in his plans. That he had a low tolerance for hiccups was becoming clear. How she knew any of this when he had revealed so little in his reaction, and her mind only now offered up hazy memories of him as a young man, she didn't know.

She offered a shrug and an airy laugh in consolation, mildly embarrassed about the whole thing though she was simultaneously unsure as to exactly why. "Otherwise, you know, I'd be all in. Despite the whole abduction…" Her cheeks were hot, likely bright pink, but it couldn't be helped so she made the joke, anyway, despite the risk that it might bring his eyes to her face, that it might mean their eyes locked again and he stole her breath again.

Of course, that is what happened. And then there was that smile again, the one that said he knew all about the strange mesmerizing power he had over her, and it pleased him.

Whether he was the kind of man who used his power for good or evil had yet to be determined.

Either way, beneath that infuriating smile, deep in his endless brown eyes, was the sharp attunement of a predator locked on its target. "Give me a week." His face may not have changed, but his voice gave him away, a trace of hoarseness, as if his sails had been slashed and the wind slipped through them, threaded it, a strange hint of something Hel might have described as desperation…if it had come from anyone other than him.

"What?" she asked.

"Give me a week to change your mind."

Hel's sympathy dried up like a desert pool. She shook her head. "No, thank you. I'm pretty set on this. And while I appreciate the seriousness, as well as the lack of intention, you did kidnap me…"

He laughed, and the sound of it eased some of the tightness in her chest. She brought a hand to the spot in the center of her breastbone, where the sensation seemed to coalesce, and rubbed as he continued, his eyes sharp on her every movement. "Give me seven days to bring you around to my plan. We want the same thing, in the end. Let me convince you."

Hel snorted. They didn't exactly want the same thing. He wanted revenge. She wanted eradication. But she didn't say that. Instead, she asked, "And if you can't? What do I get?"

His eyes lit, voice picking up a charge as he said with a shrug, "I bring you back home, forgiven—no harm, no foul. You did your part to right the wrong."

She sucked in a little breath, the only outward sign of the allure of that promise. But, clearing her mind, she shook her head and said, "My job prevents things being that simple."

He chuckled. "It's not just your job."

Hel smiled. "Agreed. My absence is likely already rather visible."

He nodded sagely and she almost laughed.

"Now, and I know this is rather unconventional, " he began, "but, seeing as how you are already 'kidnapped,' my suggestion would be to keep things simple and just remain so."

Now Hel did laugh. A lot.

Shaking her head, she wiped at the tears that escaped from the corners of her eyes. When she had collected herself, she said, "So you're suggesting I take this as an enforced holiday, if you will?"

He gave a single, firm, grave nod in response and another chuckle bubbled out of her.

"And on this enforced vacation, you're going to try and seduce me out of the deathbed vow I made to my father?" She lifted an eyebrow with the question.

He smiled, his grin quick and wicked. "If you want me to. I just said I'd change your mind, though."

Hel's blush was an immediate inferno—hot

enough that she glanced surreptitiously at her arm just to make sure she hadn't caught fire.

"You're not," he said, reading her mind.

"What?" she asked, irritation threading the question.

"On fire," he said, chuckling. "You looked worried."

"What are you talking about?" she snapped, knowing exactly what he was talking about.

"Well, you're as red as a ripe tomato and even look a little sweaty, so I only thought…"

Her mouth dropped open again. "I'm not sweaty," she said.

He inclined his head and raised his palms. "My mistake. Glistening."

There was no match for his audacity, Hel realized. No attack she could be assured he wouldn't deflect smoothly…except one.

"Yes." The word danced out of her mouth, relaxed and self-assured, while her stomach spiraled and her palms went clammy. She had the sense of things picking up speed, right before they spun out of control—the moment before the crash she knew so well from her days of high-performance racing, but it was too late to take her foot off the gas now.

Once again, his entire body stilled, his cocky smile gone for a frozen moment as he stared her dead in the eye, gaze searching and intense. Uncertainty, raw emotion and… vulnerability all poured out of the deep, soul-revealing orbs of his eyes, and in the face of it, she was nearly lost, though to what she didn't know.

She had thrown him off balance for once. It had taken offering herself up on a platter in order to do so, but she had been success-ful. But as things shifted within her, she re-alized he wasn't the only one.

"You're sure?" His eyes left no room for anything but absolute and irrefutable com-mitment.

Hel swallowed. Was she? Jenna and the king's guard could handle her absence, but could she handle the man before her? There had never been a shadow of a doubt before, but there had also never been a challenge be-fore. In fact, she'd yet to meet a challenge she wasn't a match for.

The reminder shored her when her heart was less certain.

"Yes," she answered.

Triumph lit his eyes, his grin returning, his canines catching the light streaming in through the skylights, to shine bright white and sharp. He licked his lips and she was helpless to do anything but watch, fascinated, rapt, absolutely trapped.

He pushed away from the desk he was leaning against and closed the space between them until she was forced to tilt up her head to maintain their eye contact.

Instinctively she knew not to break it, knew it would trigger a chase that she wasn't sure she was fast enough to outrun.

In truth, she wasn't sure it hadn't already begun.

He brought his hands to her jaw and ran his fingers along its stubborn line, tiny jolts of electricity shooting through her skin in the wake of their contact. She sucked in a breath and his smile reached his eyes, though it could never have been called warm.

No. Warmth was pacts and partnership.

The light that lit his eyes was triumph—cold, bright and biting.

He angled her face up, tilting it toward his even farther for greater access. His eyebrows had drawn together while his eyes stormed, both pleasure and anticipation weaving together with his win.

"Seven days. No more, no less—unless, of course, it doesn't take that long." And then he kissed her.

If she hadn't already been lost at sea, she would have sworn the earth roiled beneath her when their lips met.

Like magnets with opposite poles, they locked on contact, neither of them in control of the attractive force that held them. He plundered, of course—what else would he have done? He was a pirate.

She surprised herself, though, when she opened to the onslaught, rather than pushing him away immediately and with grand retribution—what she would have done with any other man.

Sensing the surrender in her softening, he took more. More surprise came as she welcomed his dominance, pouring her own fierce nature into it, just this one time completely unafraid of overwhelming someone else.

With his free hand he undid the top buttons and slipped his shirt over her shoulders—all without breaking the kiss.

Hel, drowning as she was in the sensations of his generous lips pressed against hers, didn't care what else he did as long as he held his line, his tongue marauding, her system reveling in this rare moment of being overpowered.

Pressing closer, he drew her body against the long length of his hard body, heedless of his sea-soaked clothing, which did nothing to cool the heat building in her veins.

As he drew her nearer, his thigh pressed against the crease of her thighs, wedging an opening between them, his wet clothes a sensual abrasion against her sensitive bare skin.

The echo of a sharp inhalation bounced around the room when he made contact with the molten core of her, and it took her mind a moment to process the fact that the sound came from her. Rational mind struggling to come back to itself, back to its home in the driver's seat of her consciousness, she tried to remember the terms of their deal and her vow and her very name, but couldn't seem to hold thought in the face of each sensory revelation.

He tasted like salted caramel on a short-bread cookie, the sweet savory combination of the one thing her mother knew how to cook that she looked forward to every holiday season. A flavor she couldn't get enough of.

He smelled like salt water and leather and rope, and something she had never encountered before but her mind told her was his skin, a scent she'd find nowhere else but here.

He completely encompassed her, hard and hot, pressing against her like a molten iron bar, reshaping her into something new.

Waves of electricity rode through the remaking of her until she couldn't be sure that she hadn't become merely a conduit—a vessel created to contain all his energy and power.

He growled and the sound rippled across her skin, leaving a trail of shivers before burrowing deep in her core.

Eyes closed, her remaining inputs heightened, overloading her system with information.

His fingertips were rough, his skin was smooth and soft. His lips were full and he was in absolute control of their kiss, not so much guiding her into new territory as grabbing her hand to take her running into the unknown, fast, heady and daring. And though the destination was forbidden, it was hard to remember that, when his invitation had been delivered in exactly her language.

Though her balance was excellent she was filled suddenly with a sense of vertigo, falling, the only constant thing his kiss as she went.

From far away, she heard the sound of laughter, growing closer as her breath turned shallow and quick. Her breasts were sensitive beacons on her chest, alert in a way she hadn't known they had the capacity to be, straining for contact she wasn't supposed to want.

Reading her mind again, his hand came to her breast, the thin fabric of his shirt serving only to enhance the erotic sensation of the searing heat of his hand cupping her swollen flesh. She gasped, and in her mind, the laughing grew louder until she could recognize whose it was.

Like an ice bucket from the underworld, her father's ghostly cackles bounced around her head, reminding her that he would always win in the end, even from beyond the grave.

Gasping, though no pleasure lingered, Hel brought the flexed side of her palm down against Drake's aorta before gut checking him with a one-inch punch to the solar plexus. Remarkably, he remained upright, taking a step back with a grunt, sucking in a breath, eyes squeezing shut, before he cracked open an eye to look at her.

She remained bent over, hands on her knees, breathing hard.

Looking up, she caught his open eye.

For a moment they simply stared at each other, Hel's bangs falling in front of her face, which she knew was a mask of exasperation. She had never been good at hiding her feelings. No amount of practice in front of the mirror could remedy her of the failing.

Then he cracked a one-eyed smile, white teeth flashing, and reached out a hand to her. "Deal?"

Hel stared at the hand offered. It was massive, rope-scarred, marked with faded tattoos, and she couldn't help herself. Rising to meet his hand with one of hers, the woman who'd grown out of the girl known for making risky wagers with the devil, the woman who had learned to put responsibility above desire, said, "Deal."

God help her.

# CHAPTER FOUR

*TRIUMPH* WAS TOO small a description for the rush of sensation in his veins. Joy, relief, rage, pride—all of them coalesced into a throbbing new emotion that threatened to overwhelm him. It wasn't closure—that would take bringing his father back, saving his mother from the hard life and exposure that had taken her early from him. But it was close. Close enough that he was tempted to let out a little of the tidal wave.

But he also didn't respond to threats, not even his own emotional ones, and so none of it escaped.

Once again, he had grasped victory from the jaws of certain defeat. And all he'd had to do to do it was catch a high-voltage current wrapped in moonglow. His plan had hinged on her, that had always been true, but he realized he'd underestimated the power that gave her all the way up to her declaration. The fact that she had a choice had been in his mind the whole time. That she might refuse had never truly crossed it.

He had come this far through relentless self-assuredness, and emerged as the natural leader in every group effort he'd been a part of. He had been irritated by the element of uncertainty she introduced into his endeavor, and yet he'd underestimated it all the same.

Her eyes had steel in them as she'd spoken. She'd been serious. He'd been prepared to break down defenses that were social—they were weak at best. He was an excellent catch and had her disdain for her father on his side. Despite the absurdity of it, he'd never imagined her walls would be of such a deep and personal nature. Nor so irrevocable.

In her gorgeous blue eyes, bright and inviting as the Caribbean Sea, he'd seen her resolution, as binding as his own promise to himself and his mother's memory. She would not be moved. And in that liquid firmament, his grand plans began to drown. He would return to Calla a failure, just as he'd arrived decades before. The admiral and captain, everything he'd done going down with the ship because in the end, he was just like his father—brought down by the d'Tierrzas.

His offer had been a desperate call to the wind—her simple *yes* the light of a lighthouse flickering to life on the shore. It had been a risky and near thing, but he'd escaped the gale force just before it tore apart his soul.

So if he'd nearly lost control, nearly let the tide of emotions break free of the dam of his control, it could be understood.

And by the way she'd responded to his kiss, her vow would be forgotten before they even arrived in Calla.

Even accounting for the sucker punch.

He grinned, allowing the expression as his mind raced ahead, plotting and planning his campaign, even as his stomach continued to roll.

The woman had an arm.

But she was naive and as clear as glass when it came to what lovers did.

She was completely ignorant of the rarity

of the thing that had sparked between them. It was a feeling even he, as experienced as any respectable sailor, had never had before. And he could use that.

With the heat of their kiss still electric on his tongue and the elation of his success throbbing in his system, he gestured for her to sit, every inch the magnanimous host.

"Would you like anything?" he asked. "The galley is well-stocked. My chef can make virtually anything."

She must have been feeling the beginning of hunger by now. A body that strong needed regular fuel. And even without the experience of sparring with her, the fact of her strength was impossible to miss when it was muscle tone that gave her body dimension, and, he observed, its hints of curves.

Had she not been the captain of the royal queen's guard of Cyrano, he imagined she might have had the same willowy slenderness that her mother and aunt had been famous for in their heyday. It had been rare for his mother to speak of the past, but when she did, her best friend, Seraphina d'Tierrza, famous beauty, featured heavily.

Like her mother, Helene was tall and long. Unlike her mother, she had filled out, and incredible strength hummed under the pretty packaging like a high-performance racer.

She lifted an eyebrow. "Anything?"

His grin grew even wider. She doubted him.

He loved it when people doubted him. Their ignorance was his advantage.

"Dragon fruit," she declared.

Throwing his head back, he laughed, the sound rich and warm and booming. The laugh was his father's, famous among those who had known him, and just another feature on the long list of traits Drake had inherited from him. Everything but his open heart, it seemed.

"Easy. Try again."

"Star fruit."

He snorted, nodding without bothering to answer.

"Pickled herring."

He tsked, crossing his arms in front of his chest and shaking his head. "I am ashamed at you, Helene. We might be high-class, but we're still sailors. Of course, we have pickled herring."

Chuckling, she challenged, "Durian."

He stopped laughing, gave her a stern frown and pointed a finger at her. "That's cheating."

She nodded, smiling, gemstone eyes sparkling like freshly cut and cleaned diamonds.

"No durian. Too smelly. Despite our spacious and luxurious accommodations, it is still a confined space."

This time she tsked at him. "And you said anything…" At ease, exactly as he'd intended, her voice was all smiles when she said, "A glass of water would be wonderful, please."

That she was comfortable enough to ask him for something was more significant than he thought she realized, but music to his ears. "Certainly." He smiled. "I don't even need to call for that."

He walked to a set of bookshelves and pressed a small button, then a shelf of books slid to the side, a quiet swoosh the only sound as the secret shelf-door revealed a crisp minibar. Filling a chilled crystal glass, he asked, "Bubbles?"

She laughed. "I'll talk it flat, thanks. Fits better with being kidnapped by pirates."

He brought the glass to where she sat on the sofa, legs curled under her, and handed it to her, their fingertips brushing at the transfer, sending little charged sparks up his arm.

The thrill of the win.

Because it was certain he would win her over to his plan. He had waited over thirty years for his revenge—there was no way it would be jeopardized by the whim of a re-formed rich girl.

"Are you hungry?" he asked after she had taken a few sips and set the glass on the end table.

"Not now, thank you." When she wasn't paying attention to them, her default manners were everything one would expect from a high-bred young lady.

He wondered if she knew that.

"I would like to know where I'm being kidnapped to, though," she continued, her questions mild and offhand as she stared out at the sea views around them.

"Calla, on the Sidran coast."

She filed the information away, the process as obvious to him as if he was the one doing it.

Known for his ability to read people, for cutting through the layers of deception and power-grabbing to discern the path of his advantage with uncanny and unparalleled accuracy, he had never encountered anyone as transparent to him as Helene.

Watching her, it was as if he could read her thoughts even as they formed in her mind. He wondered if it drove her crazy that her face showed her thoughts so clearly. He bet it did. He could picture her as a younger woman, practicing in the mirror, trying to hide her reactions.

The thought made him smile. He was willing to bet she had been adorable—purely earnest in an effort to change something that was fixed.

"Why Calla?" she asked, and in the question he heard layers.

"My home," he said, unable to restrain the pride in his voice. He had been born a duke's heir and had everything stolen from him. Then he had picked himself up, and climbed his way back to the very same position by his own strength and means. His title had been a gift from the Sidran king. None of his peers could say the same. It was unheard of.

Perhaps it was why his inner compass was so strong. He'd braved paths, both on land and sea, that other men had feared to tread—attack, loss, poverty—and not only lived to tell the tale, but also used them to catapult his way from their dark recesses to the very top. By himself. By trusting his instincts and inner guide and no one or nothing else. Growing up in the Sidran capital poor would have taught him that hard lesson, if witnessing his father's betrayal and resulting loss of everything hadn't already drilled it into the very fabric of his being.

He required Helene's participation in what was the most important campaign of his life, career and retirement, but trust was not a requirement, neither hers nor his. Compatibility, which they had in spades, and agreement, which she had given, were all that was required from her. Now that both were secured, it would only be a matter of time before they were well on their way.

However, as he took in the incredibly dangerous, barely clothed woman in his cabin, he had to admit that there was an unexpected flavor beneath revenge, and it was turning out to be a bit more…complex than he'd anticipated.

Challenge, he'd expected—she was one of the most dangerous and accomplished women in the world. Her vow was certainly a dangerous hurdle, but he was confident he could seduce her and had come to terms with the idea of making love to the daughter of a man he loathed long before setting his plan in motion—he would not have been the first man to turn the lights out and close his eyes for the greater good.

What he hadn't been prepared for was how good it would feel—not the achievement of his revenge, but its execution.

He hadn't anticipated she would feel like a live wire in his hands.

He hadn't planned on caring whether or not she was impressed with what he'd grown from the ashes of his life. But as his home came into distant view through his cabin's portholes, he realized it was the case nonetheless.

Calla—his little bay, purple-blue in the twilight, and it's palatial manor, set farther inland in the harbor, visible high above the high-tide line and built into the craggy savannah forest cliffs. Here was a fortune he had built himself.

Though he could not see them yet, ships, he knew, were docked farther into the harbor, safe and sleepy in their moorings, peacefully undisturbed. He'd worked hard to ensure his home was lovely, prosperous and pretty.

And with his ship's incredible speed, it was only a short time later that he sent the command to set anchor.

His personal assistant met them, boarding immediately with the change of clothing he'd ordered for Helene. With just seven days for his seduction, he didn't want any of it to be uncomfortable…even just for the duration of the drive to Caline, his ducal manor.

Visible from the docks, Caline, his home, jutted out from the hillside overlooking the bend in the river and the entire city of Calla, high above the city. Reaching it by foot was an uphill undertaking along an ancient trail under the best of circumstances, even if the journey was breathtakingly beautiful. Attempting it at the end of a long day, which had included an unexpected bout of sparring with one of the world's best soldiers and running headlong into her unexpected little vow, was not, however, the best of circumstances, and so he called a car for them.

Tonight he would wine and dine her in the privacy and seclusion of home, before he took her out to charm her with his city.

Helene's expression, however, upon opening the delicately packaged garment box brought by his assistant, did not suggest his seduction was off to an auspicious beginning.

She held up a simple dress—blue, flowing and long. Her lips pursed and she drew her eyebrows together, her opinion obvious, and he had to hold back his laugh.

"Not your style?" he asked, unable to keep the amusement from his voice. She had revealed multiple facets in their short time together, but this was the first he was seeing the spoiled daughter.

But she was not in the mood to be more revealing, or had recalled her manners, it seemed, because she just flared her nostrils and looked around, for a place to change he presumed.

Indicating the door that led to his closet, he held both his smile and comment. Whatever she didn't like about the dress, he wouldn't press. His seduction efforts stopped at comforting a woman over her clothing.

Clothes were a means to an end, not meant for emotional investment.

And, like everything he'd seen her in, when she returned draped in the clean hanging of the dress, she was beautiful.

His assistant had included a pair of strappy leather sandals, as he'd instructed. She couldn't arrive barefoot.

As he'd anticipated, the sandals were forgiving for his guess on size. Unlike the dress she'd worn upon their meeting, this was made of breezy cotton—local, if he was not mistaken—and would allow her far greater freedom of movement. She should be relieved.

She did not look relieved.

As lovely as she was, Grecian and elegant, he was reminded of his younger sister, Nya, on the occasions their mother had forced her to dress up.

He almost laughed, but held back, and instead offered her his arm. "Shall we?"

For a moment, he wondered if she would take it, but she did not disappoint, shrugging away whatever displeasure she had with her attire to rest her arm on his. As usual, there was a jolt on contact.

He led her onshore and into the sleek black car that waited for them.

They rode in a comfortable quiet and he realized it was the first truly settled stretch of time they'd had since their meeting. In fact, when he thought back, it was the first settled stretch of time he could remember in years.

It seemed like peace might finally be his in less than seven days. What would that feel like? He was ready to find out.

They pulled up the hill and into the curved stone driveway at Caline's entrance. She marveled as they exited the car, but he did not slow for a tour—they would have time for that tomorrow. Tonight was about rest, relaxation and recuperation, completely free of pressure. He wanted her supple and easy and off her guard before he set to work.

After they'd shared a kiss that had her redefining the word, Hel had expected Drake to launch a full-blown-seduction onslaught, assuming he would waste no time, or his newfound advantage, in his effort to budge her from her vow. Because an advantage was certainly what he'd proved he had with that kiss—he had an advantage strong enough to rip her from the shore and cast her out to sea. So she would need to remain on her guard, to take seriously the threat he posed to her defenses, as mesmerizing as he was.

She had mentally prepared for it throughout

the nerve-racking ride to the manor—nerve-racking not because the drive was treacherous or road conditions dangerous, but because the effect he had on her was amplified by being in a dark, comfortable confined space together. She would need to avoid kissing, and touching, at all costs.

If this was attraction, it was a wonder anyone got anything done. The relentless drive of her mind to focus on the object of her interest certainly explained some of her cousin's more asinine behavior when it came to his wife.

But she sensed none of that from Drake.

In fact, he was behaving as if the matter had gone from his mind entirely.

He had not tried to impress her with his manor, though the glimpses she'd caught had impressed her nonetheless as he'd all but marched her through the grand manse to a small, secluded balcony, the archway leading into it picturesquely framed by blooming flowering vines and soft twilight. Centered in the picture, as if intended for a still life or a movie scene, was a lovely round table, set for two with wineglasses, bread, cheese, charcuterie and fruit. Her stomach growled.

Drake laughed, "I had a feeling you would be hungry. We'll eat. After that, I've kept our evening simple—massages, followed by rest. Tough as you are, you've had a lot to process today." His smile was warm, friendly, with no trace of teasing fire.

The juxtaposition from his demeanor earlier—flirtatious, wild—was enough to put her off balance. Hot and cold, the unfamiliar territory was disorienting to say the least.

She was no more grounded after dinner. Yes, they'd shared a wonderful meal, enjoying surprisingly easy conversation, and a camaraderie she hadn't experienced since her academy days. But he hadn't directed so much as a flirtatious glance in her direction since they'd arrived in Calla.

True to his word, massages followed dinner, but he surprised her with no setup attempt, with each of them receiving their massages in serenely appointed private spa rooms.

And afterward, rather than pouncing when her mind was mush and her muscles relaxed postmassage, she was greeted by a friendly staff person who showed her to a peaceful room that looked out over the harbor. And she was its only occupant.

The next morning, the same kind staff member led her to breakfast, this time in another lovely dining area, with an enclosed sun porch that had views into the river canyon.

"Did you sleep well?" he asked.

For a moment, she simply took him in. He looked like he had rested, and well. His smile was as bright and sunny as the morning, his clothing fresh, his skin as alluring and velvet smooth in the daylight as it had been through the afternoon and evening before.

His eyes danced, observing her in the simple dress she'd found laid out for her this morning. Two days in a row in dresses and she was contemplating going nude. If he didn't have such an unpredictable effect on her and his wager didn't sit between them, she just might have.

This dress was a spaghetti-strapped maxi in cornflower-blue, shapeless but nicely draping…if one went for that kind of thing. Hel did not, and her face must have said so. She wore the sandals she had been given the evening before and knew objectively that the ensemble was lovely, the picture of a young woman on holiday. Still, it remained, indisputably, a dress.

"Fantastic, thank you. And you?" She refused to rise to the challenge in his eyes and mention the dress.

Gaze laughing, he said, "Very well. It's so much easier to rest knowing your dreams are on the brink of coming true."

Hel snorted, "I would think that might make it harder to sleep."

He brushed the back of her hand as he reached for the butter and said softly, "Maybe it's just your calming influence."

Hel laughed out loud. No one had ever called her influence calming. Her father had called it an embarrassment, a shame, unnatural, defiant, upsetting, disgusting and all manner of other things, but never calming.

That Drake did, as untrue as it was, soothed feathers she hadn't realized were ruffled. She might not be calm, but that had never made her unpleasant. It was nice to know someone beside her mother thought so.

"So what's on the agenda for today? A romantic beach walk? Dinner and a movie? A private boat ride down the river?"

His habitual smile only grew in the face of her sass.

"Hardly, I wasn't born common." He winked, but his words were an eerie echo of her father... and yet, from Drake, they were silly rather than cutting. "I thought we would play tennis."

She started. She couldn't remember her last game of tennis, and in truth, a match sounded...wonderful.

"After our rather active day yesterday, I thought it'd be a good way to get the kinks out," he said, putting words to her thoughts exactly.

Light, fun, easy—tennis would be perfect. And separated by a net, she wouldn't have to worry about touching.

He instructed his staff to find more appropriate attire for her and they met on the court twenty minutes later.

She'd been told all they'd have was a classic white skort and simple white halter top, but she had suspicions the close fit and short length were more intended for the enjoyment of Drake than her mobility on the court.

The match started out fast and strong. Drake had an incredibly powerful serve and precise aim. Hel was light on her feet, with a reach to boot, and the combination kept them evenly matched.

As he served for his last point, Hel was struck by his arresting physique. The man was truly a work of art, all power and heat, and it was all she could do to keep up. Something he only proved true with his serve. Diving toward the far left corner when she'd been positioned on the right, she barely missed the ball with the edge of her racket, cursing when both her body and the ball made contact with the court.

Drake was at her side in a moment, leaning over her, backlit by the sun, concern on his face.

"Are you all right?" he asked, gently probing her exposed skin.

His touch was featherlight and gentle, not in the least sexual, and yet her body reacted as if they were already in bed together, skin prickling, instantly sensitized to every caress, even just that of the warm, dry air of Calla. Their eyes locked, blue and brown meeting on a shore as old as man and woman, holding both of them at a standstill.

Secrets and deep emotions churned behind his gaze, and though she feared where such an undertow might carry her, she was tempted to dive in, anyway.

Eyes dropping to his lips, she found herself wetting her own and swallowing, suddenly thirsty, though not, she realized, for water.

She wanted him to kiss her again, she wanted him to look at her with that teasing flirtation that tempted her to forget who she was just on the chance he might let her run her fingers down his skin.

She wanted to see the look in his eyes she'd seen when they kissed—electric, intense, a little surprised. Looking up at him, far from home and completely at the mercy of the Big Bad Wolf, she had the horrifying realization that she wanted him to seduce her, and that meant she was in way over her head.

His plan was unfolding perfectly. They'd parted ways, the air charged between them, at the tennis court, and the look in her eyes had been undeniable. After an evening of rest, and a leisurely morning and afternoon, she was exactly where he wanted her: hungry for more.

The enchantment of the Calla night market was famous throughout Sidra. With its abundance of hand-painted paper lanterns and string lights, the dancing aromas of fresh-cooked local food, roasting meats and hot, sweet treats, and his talented artisans, farmers and craftspeople on display, it would be a seduction of the senses in itself.

He had worked hard to turn Calla into the prosperous, cheerful port town it had become—it could do work for him in return.

Hel smiled a blinding aristocratic smile at every vendor she met.

Somewhere along the way, she collected a patterned woven basket, which was overfilled with other free offerings from vendors as they made their way through the market.

She mesmerized everyone she encountered, despite the language difference. It wasn't a shock that she caught attention—she was movie-star beautiful and had a presence about her, was utterly confident and relaxed.

What surprised him, though, was the effort she put into it. She went out of her way to be kind to everyone she met, trying offered foods and dutifully examining every item and tasting every morsel she was presented with.

After encountering her as a fighter and then a sarcastic captive, he was mildly surprised—and a little impressed—to witness her as a gracious traveler.

But he didn't fail to notice the almost imperceptible sigh of relief and easing of her shoulders as they exited the market. She had put on a good show, but the effort had tired her, more so than any of their battles of strength and will had, which he would not have expected. The woman had incredible reserves of energy.

Together they walked along the Tela River,

outside of the market now, along the quieter row of long-established, high-end riverside restaurants. Later, after dinner, a car would meet them to take them back to the manor.

Cobblestone streets and whitewashed mud-brick walls dominated here, but bright pops of color in the forms of painted buildings and trees exploding with blossoms ensured the eye had a full buffet of delights.

The Tela was a cool whisper at their side, quiet and calm, before it opened softly into the harbor, having made its long slow curve through the city and its mad rush through the semi desert canyon valley, where wild goats and deer came down the steep cliffsides to drink from its banks.

The restaurants along the river were among the most popular and expensive in the city, their special coastal cuisine famous throughout the entirety of Sidra.

As Drake understood it, reservations were a must, and hard to come by, but he wasn't worried. Being the man who had made it all possible had its perks.

He secured them a lovely mosaic-topped

bistro table facing the night-darkened Tela, her waters inky and slick, small eddies catching the flicker of streetlamps to glisten and sparkle.

They sat on either side of the table, separated by a tasteful flower arrangement, elegant, largely rounded, long-stemmed wineglasses, a bottle of the local red and a pitcher of fresh water, picturesquely dripping condensation in the warm breeze. Drake spoke to their server.

In Sidran, his smooth baritone undulated and danced with a warmth it lacked in his mother tongue, his second language alive with the love and welcome he'd found far from home. He knew Helene didn't speak it, but appreciated the reprieve from speaking in the formal and reserved language of his early youth.

The server lapped up their presence like a flower in the sun, his demeanor that of a proprietor eager to impress an important guest. Some things required no translation.

Their dinner, however, did.

Still smiling, Drake turned to Helene. "He says he's preparing each of his specialties, which he will serve over three courses. I tried to rein him in, but as you'll undoubtedly realize on your own, any attempt to ward off Sidran hospitality is absolutely futile."

Helene smiled and for a moment he forgot why they were there, forgot that she sat across from him at a table in Calla because he had less than six full days to convince her to give up the deathbed vow she made to her father. For a moment, she was simply the bright star of a woman he was having dinner with…and that was a kind of loosening of the reins he couldn't afford.

"I haven't gone to dinner in a long time," he admitted before he could stop himself. Eyebrows drawing together, he frowned. Verbal slips were not something common in his experience, not with his kind of control. Something about her disarmed him, though—lured, or perhaps hypnotized, him into taking his hands off the wheel, at least for a moment. It was all the more pressing that he remain diligent.

A frown crossed her own expression like

a cloud, then she said, "Neither have I. Not since the academy."

That surprised him, though his research had already told him as much.

He understood being dedicated and driven, more than most, but by his age he'd learned the value of R & R. Any sailor worth his salt knew that they were certain limits the body could not overcome. The need to recharge was one of them.

"That's a long time," he said.

She nodded, taking a bite and savoring it. Everything from the fork to the swallow was slow and sensual, then she added, "I joined the royal guard straight out of the academy, and quickly realized I wanted to make captain. I had to sit for another set of exams for that, which isn't my strong suit, and pass a more rigorous physical exam. Doing all of that while on active duty didn't leave much time for socializing."

"You made captain a long time ago," he challenged. "What has your excuse been since?"

"Touché," she said, lifting a glass to him. "I made captain and everything was wonderful—the agony and uncertainty of dating far from my consciousness—until the king was assassinated and suddenly I was a brand-new monarch's chief defense."

He noted she said, "the king," and "new monarch" rather than "my uncle," or "my cousin," when she could have said either. She took pains to distance herself from her royal connection.

"Why do you do that?" he asked.

"Do what?" she said, startled out of her assassination pity party.

He almost laughed. "Refer to your family by their titles?"

She stopped mid bite, her expression as if she'd never considered the question. Setting down her fork, she stared into the distance while she thought, and he took the opportunity to do his own gazing. Candlelit shadows danced across her face, her skin smooth, expression alive. He wouldn't have to close his eyes and think of revenge with her. In fact, the idea of seeing her at all was becoming far more than a transactional idea.

Which meant he needed to recenter his

head on his mission. His goal was revenge and the end of the d'Tierrza line. They shared the same goal—therefore, she should cooperate with him and his revenge was as good as won.

When she spoke, her voice was quiet and tinged with melancholy. "I don't want to reflect badly on them."

In his chest, his heart missed a beat. A goal like that would make for a lonely world…and he could imagine where it originated. What might have begun as a war of vengeance was turning into one of liberation. All she had to do was say yes.

"I'm not sure it's possible for Helene Cosima d'Tierrza to reflect badly on anyone. Did you know you revert to impeccable manners when you're tired? That's how I know you need to rest, when you don't have the energy to be outrageous."

She laughed, as he'd hoped she would, before inclining her head. "Thank you for the pep talk, I think."

"Thanks for going on a date with me," he said, and winked. "So tell me about your friends? If you refer to your family by their titles and haven't gone out to dinner in over a decade?'"

"No, you go first. Tell me about growing up in Sidra."

He looked away, breaking their eye contact. "You don't want to hear that story. It's long and not very interesting. Your turn."

She rolled her eyes and let out a little chuckle that sounded suspiciously like a sigh. "I'm only letting you get away with that. And I eat dinner with my best friends almost every day, thank you very much. When I have free time, I like to spend it alone."

"Chatting with statues of your father?" he teased, not buying the image at all.

She snorted but conceded, "Chatting with statues of my father. There's only one, you know."

He shuddered theatrically. "That there is even one…"

She cringed. "You're right. My mother and I always say we'll have it removed."

"What's stopping you?" he asked, curious how a woman who could hate her father so much could keep such a substantial reminder of his presence around. Particularly when she had all the money and resources she could want.

She looked thoughtful for a long moment before answering. "I think it reminds us both of what we survived."

Dark words to come from a daughter.

Drake wondered, if the child they would have together turned out to be a daughter, what she would say about him when she grew up. Nothing that Helene had to say about her own father, he vowed.

"I never thought I'd have to ask this, but why did you hate your father?" he asked.

Dominic d'Tierrza had been a hateful man, every new bit of information Drake unearthed about him that much more damning, and yet he still wondered at the kind of thing that made a daughter despise her father.

Helene smiled and Drake immediately recognized it for the clever and beautiful deflection it was.

Waving her hand airily, she said, "Pick any

ten possible reasons off the list and it'd be enough, wouldn't it?"

Leaning back in his chair, he took her in, the blue dress bringing out the color of her eyes, a wonderful fit for her willowy frame, and yet somehow hanging awkwardly on her. "But I think it's more specific than that."

Shaking her head, she looked out over the dark river and said, "Sadly, no. Just a lifetime of monstrosity the likes of which you unfortunately know."

Again, he saw the deflection. By drawing the focus to his grievance with her father she hoped to refocus the conversation away from her own.

But he was more interested in what she was hiding.

"That I do," he said gravely. "But perhaps mine is not the most egregious?" He spoke casually, as if they were considering the future of a sports team.

Something sharpened in her eye, the look dangerous if used as a weapon. She hedged. "The game of comparing egregiousness never goes anywhere. Suffice to say, there were many reasons to hate my father."

"Agreed. And what was yours?"

She smiled, but if anything, the glint in her eye had sharpened further. "Like a dog with a bone. Is that where the name 'Sea Wolf' comes from?"

He shook his head. "No. Why did you hate your father, Helene?"

Snorting, she said, "Do you really want to know?"

He nodded, though he knew she wouldn't tell him now.

"He murdered my uncle and tried to murder my cousin because he was in love with my aunt and wanted me to quit my job." She kept her inflection the same, almost bored, as if none of it was important to her and, while he knew it wasn't truly the reason she hated her father, it was true, and it hurt her.

Outwardly, he remained the same, while inside, his mind and pulse raced. This fact—that her father had been behind the plot to assassinate the former King of Cyrano—was incredible international intelligence and she'd handed it to him over a dinner table by the river.

Her cheeks were flushed, and he knew she knew the implications of what she'd just said, just as he knew she was testing him with it.

From their brief time together he'd gleaned that she was loyal, dedicated to those she loved, committed to her duty and willing to be lethal in its execution. Her father's actions would have compromised every one of those core values.

But she'd hated her father long before that. She was testing him, baiting him to see if he could be distracted from digging too deep where things were too sensitive.

Like attracted like, and just like his, hers was a mature hatred, barrel-aged in a human heart for years.

Their lives had been intertwined mirrors, each marred by the scar of Dominic d'Tierrza, without either of their knowing. She was testing to see if she could distract him, like she did everyone else, even if she didn't realize it.

She wanted him to, and he wanted her off balance, so he didn't press. When it was clear he wouldn't, the light of a real, if rueful, smile lit her expression, and she said, "So when do we eat? I'm starving?"

As if the restaurant staff could hear her, they began to bring out their food. As promised, the chef had gone all out, sending succulent bites of lamb, savory vegetables, crispy fried calamari, fresh regional fish served raw with citrus slices and a melon-ball salad with no less than four different types of melons. And this was merely the appetizer course.

She'd gotten her distraction...for the moment.

Helene took bites, oohing and aahing when appropriate, humming her pleasure after each bite, though, in truth, he wondered if she truly tasted anything.

She was being a good sport about his seduction, but since their moment on the tennis court, he had yet to truly ensnare her.

He shared stories of Calla's history and his family, and asked her about her life and work, but knew he was no closer to moving her than he had been when they'd disembarked from his ship.

The chef sent out the soup and salad, followed by a resplendent dinner course, and for the moment, both he and Helene were sidetracked by the flash and flare of spicy and sweet.

When they could stuff themselves no more and the server asked if they would like to see the dessert selection, both shook their heads emphatically, waving their hands in surrender.

"I couldn't," Helene exclaimed, her glow only enhanced from overindulging.

"No, thank you," Drake said to their server, but with a smile and the promise to return and save room for dessert the next time.

The car waited for them along the river plaza, then took them up the ancient cobblestone streets of Calla toward Caline and the further pampering that awaited them there. Drake's attack plan was always direct and relentless—he didn't stop until his objective was achieved. The seduction of Helene would be no different.

Anticipating the timing, he had ordered dessert be readied following their visit to the bathhouse and massages. That should give them plenty of time to digest.

At that point, if they weren't restored enough by pure decadence, he would show her to her room and she could sleep.

And women complained that men didn't know their true needs.

This woman had the carefree aura of the soldier that didn't know when to quit. He'd had men like that under his command before.

They were assets—as long as they were managed to prevent reckless burnout.

The driver pulled into the curved entryway and parked before coming around to open the door for them.

Drake stepped out first, offering Helene his hand, a broad smile stretching across his face at the opportunity to show her more of his manor, Caline.

She raised a slender platinum eyebrow at his offered hand and took it, sapphire eyes twinkling.

Inside, he pointed out dining rooms, party rooms and libraries on their way to his private rooms, more invested than he'd like to be in what she thought of it all.

She was used to luxury, had been weaned on it, in fact, and he watched her for her reaction. Unlike the ducal estates they had both been born to, he himself had pulled Caline and Calla from the brink of collapse and ruin. He'd rebuilt and grown them with his own labor, pockets and efforts, dragging the entire estate to a level of class that he had been accustomed to. But would she think so? Would she see that, and taste it, and feel it, as she wandered the suite designed to be his sanctuary? He wanted her to.

Situated high and center in the manor, his suites featured full landscape views of Calla, from its busy bay entrance, to the rich, fertile farmland inland and upriver.

Like the great medieval structures of Europe, Caline was built from stone.

Counting his office, bathrooms, closets, workout room, meditation space, living area and large bedroom, his suite consisted of ten rooms, including a set of guest rooms where Helene would sleep—until she slept with him, that was—and comprised the greater portion of the wing.

His sister was housed elsewhere in the structure, a floor below, her rooms with river and farm views but nothing of the sea.

While she loved him, she didn't share his love of the sea and hated waiting and watching for him to come home like some tragic figure from a dirge…at least in her words. Since it had become just the two of them occupying the manor, Caline felt cavernous. Strange and echoing and far too big for a pair of adult siblings even though they'd been just three before.

His mother had had a big presence, though, dying her gray hair silver-white and keeping it in long decorated braids, wearing daring patterns and prints, unafraid to be seen, confident she'd be admired—Amira Andros had been his model for how to navigate the world. She'd had to be after they'd lost his father.

Then it had been just him and Nya and his mother. And now it was just him and Nya, the last of the Androses. Unless, of course, Helene was agreeable.

In his common room, the decor was simple, but each and every item was of the highest quality, from his leather sofa, to the sleek built-in entertainment centers, which blended seamlessly with his still, watery aesthetic. And while no one would think to describe the room as sea-themed, there were hints of his passion and calling everywhere in the space—an original from Picasso's Blue Period, an intriguing piece of smooth, polished driftwood to bring a piece of his private island, Yancy Grove, to Calla, a subtle wave of Chihuly glass in the same swirling blues and grays of the Mediterranean during a storm, low-profile furniture and vast windows filled with open sky. Everywhere he went, he took the sea with him.

"It's lovely," she whispered, voice low.

Caught off guard by the husky thickness of her voice after going so long without words, he started.

"Thank you," he said, inclining his head. "I take my sanctuaries seriously."

A soft smile, gentle and distracted and completely new to him, lifted the corners of her lips. "I can imagine…"

A wicked grin lit his expression "What else can you imagine?"

He hadn't meant to tease her, to flirt or lure. Not yet. But then he'd watched her explore his space and see him in it.

She snorted. "Not what *you're* imagining," she retorted.

"And what's that?" he asked, keeping his face as innocent as his question was leading.

"I think we both know," she said, lifting an eyebrow.

He shook his head. "I haven't the slightest idea what you're implying."

"I'm sure."

"Bathhouse? Another massage? Dessert?"

Her mouth dropped open. "I can't believe you can even think of dessert yet. I'm still so stuffed I can barely move. But…" Her eyes took on a speculative look.

"What?" He asked, eager for her to make another request of him, eager to once again give her what she wanted—the surest means to unlocking a heart that he'd yet to find.

Looking around, she said, "I'd love to play a game of poker."

It was the last thing he expected her to ask, and absolutely perfect. Innocent that she was, she didn't realize the doors she was opening, but he did. That she'd chosen a tool he loved so well—poker—felt like a sign that things were looking up for his little plan.

Snapping his fingers, he smiled. "Done. Anything else?"

She nodded, plucking the fabric of her dress between her thumb and forefinger. "How can I get rid of this dress?"

# CHAPTER FIVE

"EASILY," HE SAID with a smile.

He could get her whatever she wanted.

Much like her father had always been, Drake was a king in his kingdom. Hel was increasingly wondering what was going on with her. It wasn't the first time she'd seen the similarities between Drake and her father—in their complete dominance, in their utter assuredness in their own way, in their ability to reduce her to emotions and reactions. And yet she was here with him, had chosen to go along, was challenging him even now to sit with her, get closer and more personal than they should, play a game that acted like a superconductor to sexual tension.

Outside, she had the wherewithal to make a joke about her dress.

Inside, her blood thrummed like a live electrical current rather than something as mundane as human ichor.

She was playing with a box of matches beside a powder keg—walking a delicate tightrope while the metaphoric wind kicked up.

But really, she hated dresses.

Sending word to the staff through his watch, he looked up at her and her breath caught, but he just asked, "What are you looking for and what size?"

"Tank top and shorts, and a small, please," she said.

He relayed her request and asked also for a deck of cards, then said, "That will be everything, thank you."

He might have had his aristocratic life stolen from him, but he certainly hadn't lost any of its nature. And for that, she was grateful. That anything remained of him after what her father had done was a wonder. That he was still—as more and more memories resurfaced, jogged loose from her time with him—so much the same young man she'd once known was nothing short of miraculous. That must have been what it was that so captured her attention about his eyes—they revealed that the same honorable, brave and kindhearted boy she'd looked up to as a child remained in the man.

Faster than she would have assumed possible, they had not only the cards, but also the change of clothes.

Her instructions had been taken quite literally. Drake handed her a plain white tank top in lovely soft cotton and a pair of black shorts. Both items were of high quality and very small.

Entering the bathroom he'd pointed out to her, Hel quickly stepped out of the dress, replacing it with the top and shorts.

Both fit, though that fit would be better described as high-performance workout wear than loungewear.

The shorts were the crevice-creeping type and the tank top hit her just below the belly button, but they were better than a dress. In these, at least, she could move.

She stepped out of the bathroom and found him waiting for her, coffee table and cushions set up for their game.

Eyes locking with his, she couldn't miss the appreciative light that lit in his gaze as he took in her attire, or do anything to stop the strange tightening of her skin in reaction.

He hadn't brought up their kiss, or the fact that she'd punched him, or their moment on the tennis courts, or really any of their physical encounters, nor had he made any further moves, all of which implied that, despite the obvious wine-and-dine attempt and his words to the contrary, he respected her vow.

Now, she just needed to stop feeling disappointed by that fact. It was a good thing— it meant she could relax and actually enjoy this unplanned vacation by smashing the gorgeous man at her side in poker.

He might have had seduction on his mind with the picturesque market and decadent dinner, but to Hel, the true seduction was the downtime. He'd told her to treat the week as an enforced vacation, and that's what she planned to do.

Not that she intended to cooperate with her own seduction. She simply hadn't had the opportunity to relax in so long.

She couldn't remember when. And while they would be worried back home, undoubtedly, she had absolute faith that her friend and fellow guard Jenna could handle her absence.

She also couldn't remember the last time she'd played poker. It was one of the things she missed about what she now realized were her carefree days at the academy. Back then she hadn't seen things in such a positive light.

They played Texas Hold'em. He dealt. She made no comment, and merely smiled when he began handing out cards.

He lifted an eyebrow and smiled back, a wild and mischievous charge thrumming between them.

Sixty hands and two hours later, while she hadn't smashed him, it was clear who the real shark was.

"Merciless," he said, tired, but relaxed in a way he hadn't been at any other point in the evening.

It was all she could do to keep her eyes off him.

The velvet cream darkness of his skin was unlike anything she had ever encountered, and she found herself filled with the most curious urge to reach out and touch it, to run her fingertips lightly along his jaw, his arm, along the edge of his hip and down his thigh…

"Now, now, Helene. What are you thinking?" His grinning question interrupted her with a start and she let out a small gasp.

His dark gaze shot to her lips, moistened and parted, and for a second, they were caught together.

And then they weren't. Then she was crossing the table and sitting on his lap, a ghost in the shell of her body that moved like a strange automaton, driven by a primal code.

He seemed to have respect for her vow.

She, it seemed, didn't.

A part of her observed from a place of panicked remove, trying in vain to put a stop to the chain of events.

The rest of her made the first move. Or was it the third move? She'd lost count. It didn't matter. It was too late to turn back.

She kissed him and he smiled into it, opening to her exploration with smooth ease, every inch her match.

For a woman who had always considered herself a solitary issue, it was a novel concept—to fit together with another human being so perfectly it seemed only divine design could have created it. Or at the very least, the longest odds the galaxy had ever seen, that random chance would construct two tiny specks, meant to join, in the infinite vastness of the entire universe.

With the exception of Queen Mina and her cousin, whose random stars had truly aligned, she didn't even believe in love like that. To feel it, alive and beating, and turn away felt like sacrilege.

Though to call resisting what was between them—mired in murder and vengeance and dangerous gambles as it was—sacrilege felt a little self-aggrandizing, no matter that the pressure of her lips against his was exquisite torture she never wanted to end.

Her body was an unyielding weapon, her very form a tool she kept in smooth order, yet now it was in charge, begging for his touch in all the silent ways women's bodies knew how...even when the woman did not.

Her breasts pressed into his chest, growing heavier, her nipples pebbling on contact. Her breath became erratic—deep, then shallow, then catching—as his fingertips trailed down her neck and farther to cup each soft peak in his hands.

She moaned when his thumbs found her nipples, running lazy circles around them while he took control of her mouth. Her breasts ached beneath his manipulations, the lightest touches making her gasp.

Her lips parted, her body yearning and straining toward him without her knowledge, a hot, heavy and needy siren song she didn't know she was singing.

With a growl he swept her up, and she wrapped her legs around his waist. Carrying her to his bed, he lay her down on her back, before pulling back from their kiss.

"I want to see you."

His command was rough, but she only smiled, shaking her head, a teasing gleam lighting her eyes. Whatever controlled her now was more daring than she, because when she opened her mouth and spoke, her voice was thick and heavy and laden with things she had never done before, even if her honor insisted as she replied, "My vow."

He leaned down over her, coming to kiss the sensitive spot behind her ear, and whispered, "There's so much ground to explore between here and breaking it…"

She shivered beneath him—her curiosity was as piqued as her pleasure.

Kissing a trail down her neck, he found another treasure trove of nerve endings along her collarbone, his hand reaching for the hemline of her T-shirt. Lifting it, his knuckles brushed along the smooth, taut skin of her abdomen, and she shivered, the sensations rippling across her skin in erotic waves.

She wore no bra and he palmed her breast without a barrier. She arched into his hand with a breathless gasp. Pulling back, he made quick work of removing her top before taking off his own shirt. Her eyes widened, lighting with greedy hunger as the tip of her tongue moistened her lips.

No longer able to tolerate the space between them, Helene pressed into him, skin-to-skin, her body responsive and needy. And then his mouth returned to her breasts.

While he feasted, his hand traveled back down the plane of her belly and farther, reaching beneath the waistband of the shorts she wore.

She was as hot and wet as a tropical hurricane, and though she didn't know where the knowledge came from, she knew that traveling through the eye of this storm would be one amazing ride.

But she was trusting him not to take them too far.

He slid his finger inside of her and her entire body clenched around him, motionless and tight for a moment, before she fell back in a heap of pulsing woman, her inner walls throbbing and squeezing around his finger, while she moaned and shuddered.

He showed her no mercy, pressing and circling the sensitive bud, overseeing it all every time the waves seemed to slow.

Only when she could truly take no more did she fall back against the bed, boneless.

He grinned down at her as she was lying there, catching her breath.

And then he set to work pulling her shorts down over her hips.

She remained boneless as he did, lifting her hips only when he was ready to slide them down. She smiled at him, the expression slightly askew and silly.

"I'm not sure you're going to be able to get much more out of me." Her words were giddy, dazed and confused.

Expression wolfish, he said, "Oh, I think you'll be surprised." His lips touched the supple skin of her stomach.

Tensing, her hand fluttered to his shoulder, and he smiled against her skin. He paused, kissing and teasing her torso, exploring the sensitive skin beneath her breasts and along her rib cage, experimenting with touch and sensation until she forgot all about her earlier tension. And when her mind was thoroughly lost in the chills undulating across her skin, he resumed his journey, gently kissing his way to her core.

When he arrived, she stilled, her senses intent and alert, desperate to know what would come next, but no longer hesitant. She was in too deep for that now.

His lips made contact and she cried out his name, her hips flying off the bed. In response, he gripped her, his fingers pressing into the firm flesh of her thighs and behind, easily catching and holding her weight in his hands.

Then he ran his tongue around the outer edge of her opening, slowly, deliberately, agonizingly slow, and when his circle was completed, he plunged his tongue inside her, and she dove over the edge.

Her body convulsed like a storm, hot waves of her pleasure pulsing, while her breath came in ragged gasps. His kiss had shaken her to her core. This—this had shattered her into a million pieces and melted each and every one of them.

Congealing back into her former self, she couldn't stop the goofy grin.

He hadn't been lying. There was a long stretch between celibacy and not pregnant, and it seemed like a week of enforced vacation with Drake might be the perfect time to explore it. His eyes—easy, warm and cocky, as always—suggested he was up for the adventure.

She just had to remember that he was also up for crossing that outer boundary. He was exciting and thrilling and more beautiful with every passing moment, but like all of the aristocratic men she'd known in her life, he had an agenda.

An agenda that had nothing to do with her and everything to do with her name and her father.

The thought cast a shadow over her lingering pleasure as she sat up. Sliding off the bed and pulling up her shorts, she marveled that so much could shift without getting completely undressed.

In fact, he was fully clothed, if disheveled.

Which was convenient, as someone chose the moment to swing the door open exuberantly.

Hel quickly scanned the newcomer, noting that she was a statuesque young woman with deep umber skin whose proportions presented serious competition to Queen Mina's newly famous curves. The young woman's hair was deep black and hung to her waist in hundreds of tiny braids. Each one was perfect and glossy, many of them decorated with thin golden rings and tiny gold cuffs that sparkled where they caught the light.

It was little Nya, all grown up and gorgeous. And, based on the stunned expression on her face, she had not been expecting her brother to be entertaining company.

"I— Oh, goodness. I'm so sorry!" she gasped.

Hel blushed—she wouldn't have been able to help that if her life depended on it, to her shame—but she didn't cringe or flinch in the face of being caught. She'd never be a spy, but she'd learned how to make up for her weakness by being better than everyone else at her job. And, as long as they weren't deadly, she'd learned to see embarrassments and stumbling blocks, such as being caught playing with fire when your honor was on the line, as opportunities to learn and grow.

This situation, for example, was an excellent reminder of just how quickly things burned out of control when touching got involved.

Touching was most definitely not safe, not when the mere brush of skin set them off like it did.

Hel shook her head, opening her mouth to say that she should be the one to apologize, when Drake cut her off, turning to Nya with frustration in his voice. "Helene, Nya. Nya, Helene. Helene and I have some serious matters to come to a conclusion on and not much time to do it so I am taking her to Yancy Grove. We'll sail on the *Ibrahim*."

"Now? It's past eleven o'clock at night," Nya pointed out.

Hel, to whom this was also news, lifted an eyebrow.

"Yes, immediately. We'll be gone no more than a week, Nya. Stay out of trouble."

It was a clear dismissal, and his sister, desperate to get out of the room, was going to heed it. She smiled the same half smile her brother had and said, "I always try," then shot Hel a final apologetic wave and left the room.

The room was quiet, neither of them speaking, the weight of what they'd done heavy and delicious all at once, until Hel couldn't take it anymore.

Forcing a half smile, she tilted her head, brought a hand to her chin and pondered. "I wonder what she wanted." She had always been happy to play the clown if it meant lightening the mood, a trait she'd learned from her mother.

Just as it'd always worked with her mother, Drake smiled at her, the expression warmer and more rooted than her attempt had been, and he reached a hand out to her.

She didn't know whether it was because of the incredible adventure of the day they'd shared, or because she knew they'd been heading in a direction she'd had no control over and was still shaken from it, but she took it.

For a moment, she thought he might pull

her close, but then he released her hand to grab a jacket from a closet.

"You're going to need another layer when we get down to the harbor."

Smiling, she slipped the high-quality, but much-too-large waterproof jacket over her body, swimming in it ridiculously like some kind of haute couture runway model.

"You're always trying to get me in a dress," she teased.

He laughed. "I will deny it to my dying breath. We both know I am trying to get you *out* of your dress."

Cheeks heated, Hel laughed, her heart lighter than it had been since before his sister had come in.

A few minutes later, a car was driving them back down the long hill from Caline, into the lovely streets of Calla.

There, Drake led her by the hand to an exquisite sailboat docked at the end.

Gleaming silver and wood and fiberglass shone in the growing moonlight. It was large enough that it likely boasted all the necessary amenities for a long trip, but small enough for a single man to manage on his own. It was freedom fabricated.

In the sweeping script at its bow was the name of his father, *Ibrahim*. Hel suspected this boat meant more to him than even the larger *Nya II*, which he'd used to…borrow her.

Standing on the dock at his side, wonder at his sailboat a wedge in her throat, she searched for the shield of her nonchalance. "So. We're going to Yancy Grove, are we?"

He laughed, seeing through her act in a way no one else ever had, not even those closest to her. "We are. Yancy Grove, my secluded private island."

Hel raised an eyebrow. "You have a private island? What happened to the poor sob whose inheritance was stolen?"

Again his laughter rang out, skipping across the lapping waves like a perfectly smooth stone. Shaking with it, he asked her, "Now what kind of self-respecting pirate would I be if I didn't have a private island where I stash my booty?" he asked.

Watching him, his deep brown eyes flashing in the moonlight, the sound of the water lulling her into dropping at least some of her shields, something strange and delightful fluttered in her throat and she smiled at him, then repeated his question, "What kind of pirate indeed?"

And when he jumped on board and reached a hand out to help her up, Hel surprised herself once again by taking it.

# CHAPTER SIX

DRAKE STEERED HIS beloved *Ibrahim* out of Calla Bay, which rested so quiet now that no one in their right mind would have believed it had once been a chaotic playground for modern-day pirates.

Hel sat on the dash to his right, her long legs curled up beneath her as she watched the night dark sea blur into the stars ahead. Impossibly hungry again, she chewed an apple that she had found upon searching the galley after they'd set off.

She had offered him one, but he had declined.

As an admiral, he had been in command of many ships, and as a sailor before that had long become used to sailing with company, but it was a novel experience sailing with a companion. Especially on the *Ibrahim*. This was his private vessel.

"I told you, you don't need to stay up," he repeated.

She crunched into her apple, then replied, "And miss sighting land on my very first pirate island? No way."

He chuckled.

"Well, it's lucky for you, then, that we'll arrive at Yancy Grove in less than an hour."

She let out an exaggerated sigh. "Good. I was afraid we might have to sleep *here* tonight."

This time he laughed outright. She spoke like the *Ibrahim* was a tin can, rather than a sixteen-foot luxury yacht, personally designed to meet his every whim and provide the highest level of comfort.

He loved the boat only slightly less than his late mother and his sister.

"No. Our accommodations will be regrettably more stationary for the night."

"You say regrettable, I say acceptable," she retorted and he reflected that it was a good thing they were alone, with no possibility of interruption, for more reasons than seduction.

She was far too good at putting him at ease.

It was becoming a struggle to remember that it wasn't mutual admiration that held them together.

He watched her while she watched the stars, her strange moonglow even brighter in contrast to the pure black of the starlit sky.

She fit there, sitting on his dash bathed in the lights of the night, as solemn and motionless as a freshly carved and diamond-painted masthead.

She was certainly as unearthly beautiful as the mermaids and Valkyries that graced the bows of so many antique boats, including some he'd had the pleasure of sailing. *La Sirenita*, *Tristan's Wake*, *Cassiopeia*... Each one was a grand dame of his past. Helene and the children they would have were his future.

A future he'd been dreaming of since the day he'd washed up on shore, choking salt water and sand, remade and reborn out of the ashes of personal tragedy, though he'd only realized that was true when they'd lowered his mother into the ground, the land welcoming her solid and firm and eternally far from home.

It hadn't been right, that his family had been the one to suffer while a criminal lived in splendor. It wasn't right and he was determined to balance the scales. Helene was the key to that, in a plan that required he remain removed and rational. He must maintain control.

His grip tightened on the helm but his voice was even when he said, "It's a shame your first sight of Yancy Grove will be at night. Moonlight doesn't do it justice."

She looked at him over her shoulder, the move somehow erotic despite the fact that nothing about her demeanor spoke of sex.

Still draped in his jacket and once again barefoot, she should have looked like a child in adult's clothing. Instead, she was a creature of endless limbs, the quintessential irascible waif. For a woman of her height, to achieve the effect was no small feat.

"What's it like?" she asked, her words direct, like her cerulean stare. It was a trait he liked about her.

For a moment, he was lost in the sea of her eyes. Then he answered, "Long, creamy stretches of near-white sand." His gaze took in her limbs hungrily, recalling the supple lengths of milk-pale skin pressed against his head while he feasted on her. His trousers tightened, but he continued his perusal, his gaze trailing up to meet the incredible gemstones of her eyes. "The water is crystal clear," he added. "Ranging from the deepest sapphire-blue to turquoise." Then he looked up, eyes locking on the starlit strands of her short silver-blond hair. "The surf shimmers, glittering both day and night, whether it laps beneath the sun or moon."

Her breath held as he paused, her attention fixed on his lips.

His mouth quirked up. All he had to do was get her alone and give her enough time to stare at him and she seduced herself. The fact that he got the distinct impression this was a new phenomenon for her wasn't hard on the ego. Even if it made other things hard.

Each encounter with Helene had been electrifying, unprecedented and edifying. Helene was an innocent, not simply to physical pleasure, but romance, as well. And, he suspected, attraction in general. It was clear in the way she threw herself wholly into the throes of the moment. How she was caught, mesmerized by her own reaction to him. How there was a vulnerability in her approach that existed in nothing else he'd seen her do.

Existed for him alone.

A tremor went through him at the thought, strange and tangled and possessive, but there was no time for it. No time for poetry and no time for... There was no time for any of it. His future was on the line. Justice was on the line.

He licked his lips, and she swallowed and he told himself the rush that surged through his veins was triumph rather than a trap. "Amongst the dunes," he said, voice thick, "palm trees sway in the breeze. Tall, slender, supple..." he continued, his voice dropping, luring her to lean closer.

She took the bait, scooting her body closer to the helm, and he continued. "In the sunlight, its beauty is nearly blinding, it's so bright and crisp."

She had turned around to face him, still

cross-legged, attention snared. "When did you find it?"

Drake smiled at the memory. "By accident, a long time ago. We were retreating."

A little laugh escaped her. "I wasn't sure the term was in your vocabulary…"

His smile widened, as he let her see hints of his bite in the expression. "I said it was a long time ago. And as it turned out, our retreat turned into the discovery and claiming of a heretofore unknown island, as well as the opportunity to stage an ambush and collect our first prize…on behalf of King Amar of Sidra, of course."

"How efficient."

He inclined his head. "I try."

"And humble, too."

He shrugged, about as humble as a house cat. "It doesn't pay to get ahead of yourself…"

"Certainly not," she agreed, rolling her eyes. "How lucky that you stumbled upon a completely uninhabited, previously undiscovered island. In the Mediterranean."

He laughed at her dry words. "I never said undiscovered, I said unknown—to Sidra. It falls just this side of the edge of Sidran waters, hence being left alone by the rest of the sea, but it's use predates the establishment of Sidra. Until my men and I landed there was no modern record of its existence. After our report, an official review revealed that the island had been used as an ancient military port but had fallen out of use after the country's first wave of modernization."

"Hmm-m-m…" She stretched out the hum of the *M* and he felt the thrum of the vibration all the way in his bones. "Ancient military outpost. So, structures?"

He nodded, pleased with her quick mind. "Yes. And a bit more glamorous than what the men and I were used to as professional sailors. Ancient generals had it good."

She grinned, and in it he sensed her solidarity with those ancient military men, even though they wouldn't have recognized her place among them.

He was under no such illusions. Having encountered her in action, he knew without a doubt that the woman at his side was a warrior, through and through. She didn't just live—she attacked existence. She had been that way as a child, he recalled now, as more and more memories of her as a girl returned, visions of her long hair trailing behind her as she trailed behind him.

The long hair was gone. The girl, however, was surprisingly alive in the woman at his side.

The heir to his greatest enemy.

The memory of Dominic d'Tierrza brought along with it the usual surge of rage—it was the beast that had hunted him from the moment he'd washed up on that shore thirty years ago. One he would be free of with the achievement of his vengeance.

All he needed to do was get the agreement of the tall, bright and deadly woman at his side. A part of him resented that he needed even that much. But he was making progress...

He guided them through the slight change of direction that would take them on the current that led to Yancy Grove. The more dominant current, which veered north sharply, took ships out of sight of the island.

Then he reached out to take her by the back of the head and draw her closer. Her eyes widened but she merely watched him, body taught, ready to strike should he push her further than she wanted to go.

The knowledge of her coiled strength, more than a match for his own, did not deter him in his intention. She was strong, but he was dominant and relentless.

Her hair felt like cool silk slipping through his fingers, her skin beneath it faintly chilled.

She stared him directly in the eyes as the space between them disappeared, her lips parting slightly as their inevitable contact neared.

And then she was gasping, pulling back abruptly, her eyes widening into blue saucers.

Turning quickly, the sight that met him had him letting out a breath of relief.

No enemies or obstacles graced the horizon, just Yancy Grove rising in the night.

Like the woman at his side, even in the darkness, Yancy Grove glowed.

Against the backdrop of the black sky, the island was an endless stretch of moonlit sand, speckled with palm trees and dune grasses, their silhouettes stark against the white cliffs. From the cliffs, a fortress rose, carved out of the very hillside to tower multiple stories above it. The whitewashed stone walls, arched windows and gorgeous natural accents were vibrant and visible—both at a distance in dim lighting.

Simultaneously ancient and timeless, the fort at Yancy Grove was beautiful and beautifully defensible.

If love at first sight was the instantaneous knowledge that your heart had found its home, then that was what Drake had experienced as he'd scrambled on the beach and looked up at the cliffs that long ago day.

He felt the same strange calm to this day that had fallen upon him that moment when Yancy Grove had come into sight. Calla was his pride, but Yancy Grove was his joy.

Helene's eyes were glued to the island growing on the horizon.

"It's stunning," she whispered.

He stood taller, his chest expanding at her praise.

Like Calla, with Yancy Grove, Drake had taken what fortune he had been given and run with it.

Bit by bit, he had modernized and updated the fort, retrofitting it with all of the modern conveniences he'd become accustomed to as the Duke of Calla, as well as the high-tech security and telecommunications capabilities he demanded as retired admiral Drake Andros and internationally known privateer, the Sea Wolf.

Yancy Grove began their relationship, opening her arms wide and succoring him as a pup, and he maintained it, caring for her with the ardent devotion of a young lover.

"We will dock and walk up to the fortress. I do not keep a staff here as this is my private getaway."

Her reply was droll. "I think I can handle a walk."

He laughed. "We'll see if you're still singing the same tune when you see the hill." He joked, but in truth, he was impressed with her. The only child of his greatest enemy she may be, but the woman had stamina. She had kept pace with him through every unexpected hurdle the day had thrown at her, including him. He was man enough to acknowledge that there had been a number of times throughout the day that she hadn't merely kept pace, but had surpassed him.

Noting her proud bearing and the light of excitement in her eyes, he didn't think she was anywhere close to her edge, either. Not for the first time, she reminded him of a bolt of lightning masquerading as a human, not powered by an internal battery like poor unfortunate mortals, but the source of power herself.

He docked the *Ibrahim*, meticulously preparing it for rest before he and Helene disembarked. The island was silent, the warm breeze a permanent and welcome friend, carrying the scents of sea and salt.

They also walked in silence, her long legs easy match for his stride. She was tall and strong, and yet undeniably a woman, even in the darkness, dressed in his clothing, feet youthful and bare.

"You've got a thing against shoes," he observed.

Startled out of stargazing by his statement, she looked down at her feet before looking back up to him, a lopsided grin turning her classic beauty impish. "I think it might just be the barefoot sea-faring life for me."

She had a siren in her blood. He was sure of it. That or she was some kind of mystical creature, a selkie, a shield maiden, a mermaid given legs. What else could explain the way his jacket flowed around then hugged the firm lines of her lithe legs, or how when she smiled, her wide coral lips revealed a mouthful of pearlescent teeth, charming and sharp at the same time, ready to take a bite out of whatever life threw at her.

That light in her eyes was an unquenchable thirst for adventure and it could make it all too easy, if he allowed it, to lean over and set off a series of aches that began below the belt and ended with his plans embedded in her womb.

She had been drawn from a sailor's dream, but like all the great sea tales, she sprang from the loins of hell. And every time he touched her, she opened like a flower created only for him.

"I find it hard to picture you this way full-time," he lied.

She brought a hand to her heart. "You mock my dreams!"

He couldn't stop his smile, even knowing she'd commanded it from him as they rounded the curve that led to the fort's entrance.

This time, she didn't gasp at the encounter, but stopped in her tracks, mouth dropping open.

He laughed, pleased more than he cared to examine at her reaction to the project of his heart.

If the fort at Yancy Grove was breathtaking at a distance, it was a masterpiece up close. Lit up against the night sky, its walls were blinding white, butter-smooth and hand-painted for over a century, the layers of paint freshened regularly. Smooth curves dominated the architecture, with abundant built-ins tucked away for every possible convenience:

reading nooks, sea-view benches, dining alcoves, boundless bookshelves. Vibrant patterned pillows and cushions in intricately designed handwoven cases fit wherever one might imagine lounging and gorgeous rugs in one-of-kind patterns adorned gleaming hardwood floors, lending softness and color to the crisp beauty of the interior. The floors were such a deep rich brown they were almost black, and shone to the point of reflection.

An assortment of embroidered and beaded slippers waited for them in the foyer. Drake reached for a rare plain tan pair while Helene looked back and forth from the sparkling interior to the slippers.

Finally, she said, "I'm going to ruin your slippers."

Drake laughed. "Don't worry about it. There's plenty more where those came from. They're meant for company, donated afterward if the condition is still good. I buy enough from a shoreline family to keep them in the black for the year."

With the matter settled, she reached greedily for a pair in royal blue, embroidered with gold threading in the shape of sea birds.

She clearly had a thing for blue. And the sea.

The thought brought a smile to his lips.

She would adore the island in daylight.

Their feet adorned, he led her on a tour of the converted fort, locating each of the necessary items, including the four luxurious spa bathrooms, outdoor shower, both kitchens and all three kitchenettes. Then he showed her the superfluous stuff—the saunas, the workout room, the home theater, each of the six guest rooms, both libraries, the various patios, the war room, the wine cellar and, finally, all eleven indoor pools.

The pools were the gems of Yancy Grove, the features of true brilliance amongst a sumptuous sea—diamonds on a silk cushion. Unlike indoor pools common to million-dollar homes, these were hand-hewn, like the walls, literally built into the room, seamlessly integrated and oriented—either starring in or supporting the overall design of the room. Each pool was accented with features to complement its intended use, whether soaking, sky viewing, swimming, drinking, or playing. Seating, places to balance glasses, long wide lanes and broad wall cutouts were common sights among the pool rooms, as were intricate hand-tiled mosaics featuring dazzling designs made from brilliant ceramics and glittering gemstones.

"Amazing," she breathed, eyes glued to the design before her. It was the last of the pool rooms, and his favorite. This pool was designed for stargazing, its mosaic a celebration of the heavens, boasting an incredible blue ombré sky dotted with stars of golden filigree, arranged in imitation of the view above, constellations and all.

A curved archway opened up to the great yawning sky, the pool's edge drawing nearly to its gate. Alongside the pool were long cushioned benches, their fabrics and designs subdued and minimal compared to the rest of the rooms—whites and pale blues repeated in simple patterns. Made from the same material as Turkish towels, each pillow's interior was waterproof with absorbent, moisture-wicking cases, ensuring comfort as one drifted between soaking and lounging in the moonlight.

"I want to get in," she said, her eyes hungry as she took in the clear water.

He laughed, gesturing toward the pool with an open palm. "By all means." He was fine letting Yancy Grove and the sea do the work of seducing her for him. They had stolen his heart long ago.

She looked at him then, her brow furrowing. "I don't have a suit."

He shrugged. "Haven't we moved past modesty by this point?"

She quirked up a golden eyebrow in response and said, "Interesting that a man with slippers available in every size and eleven pool rooms does not have spare swimming attire."

Grinning unapologetically, he said, "You got me. Ah, well then. I suppose I must tell you about the storage closet full of an assortment of guest clothing."

Laughing, she crossed her arms in front of her chest and nodded. "I suppose."

He gave her directions and she was off, her one-track mind focused on its goal, and he smiled after her.

Though he had researched her thoroughly, she was turning out to be different than he had expected—transparent one moment and inscrutable the next, electric fire and cold logic, utterly a soldier to her core. Unlike her father, she was courageous, committed, willing to risk herself for anything greater, or, perhaps, anything at all.

Following her lead, he exited the star pool, heading for his own rooms rather than the guest closets.

The air in the room was still, hushed and undisturbed since his last visit to the island, only weeks before. Quickly finding a pair of trunks, he slid them on, not caring of the style or design, instead more eager to get back to his target, so to speak.

He found her in the star pool, already in the water. To no surprise, she had chosen a blue swimsuit. Deep navy, it was a simple bikini, of high quality, because that was all he bought, handmade and local. It fit her well, highly adjustable as it was, being mostly comprised of string.

As she had aboard the *Ibrahim*, she watched the stars above, her back to him, her skin pale and shining, the swatch of dark, thick, water-resistant fabric stretching across the toned cheeks of her derriere, held in place by perfect ribbons tied at either side of her hips.

If there was a part of him that was forever young, it was the part that rose up to whisper to him how easy it would be to pull one of those strings, to free the gallant cloth from its tremendous burden of covering her creamy curved behind.

"You didn't say the pool was heated," she said on a moan, breaking into his prurient thoughts.

Nothing about her demeanor indicated that she had become aware of his reentrance, yet she knew he was there.

Smiling, he answered, "It didn't seem important to you either way."

Turning around with a smile, she froze him in place with a look. "I was willing when it was cold water. I am compelled now that I know it is warm. I am never leaving." She drew her words out like a purr and he felt himself stir, even as something in him cautioned that he had tested her far enough tonight.

Ignoring the voice, he smiled, his mouth and tongue working, though his mind was still mildly stunned by the sight of her breasts pushing against the small triangles of fabric, as determined in their effort to press the bounds, it seemed, as their owner. It was her smile, though, unguarded and bright, transporting him to times before he'd learned the world was hard—times he thought he'd long ago forgotten—that truly held him in place. "I'll have to keep that preference in mind," he muttered, trying but unable to shake off her glamour.

He wasn't sure how it happened, but she made him laugh. Regularly. Not the laugh he was in control of—his father's loud, booming, carefree laugh that he'd mimicked his whole life—but the genuine amusement of a man.

"Why do you call it Yancy Grove?" she asked.

\* \* \*

The answer was as easy as it was painful. "We named it for our friend who didn't make it back from its discovery."

The frown that furrowed Helene's face, shadowing her eyes in the process, was one of understanding. "I'm sorry."

Drake shook off the sympathy. "It was a long time ago. Yance, Malik and I graduated from the naval academy and entered the king's navy the same year. It was Prince Malik's first command. We were outgunned by a human trafficker and Yance was hit and we were boarded."

Helene's eyes widened. "You lost the ship?"

He shook his head. "I didn't say that. We were boarded. We fought them off, but Prince Malik was nearly killed and ended the battle unconscious. I led the retreat. The luck of the sea was with us that day, but even though we discovered the island, we lost Yancy. We buried him in the fort's courtyard grove and named the island in his honor."

Moving quietly through the water, she came to his side and placed a hand on his shoulder.

"I'm sorry." The blue of her eyes, as tempestuous as the ocean, was deep and serious, and he was once again reminded that a soldier hid beneath the pretty mask.

Not just a soldier. A commander. Someone who could understand this particular pain. The kind that gnawed and ate at you from the inside, clawing to get out but too tender for the light.

"I miss him still," he said. "But that was a long time ago. Long before duty called Malik back to the capital and I retired."

"You mentioned he was a prince?"

He smiled, a teasing glint coming to his eyes. "Helene, are you angling for an introduction?"

Her snort in response was the furthest thing from being blue-blooded he could imagine, and yet, coming from her, the noise was upper-crust. "Spare me. I just wanted to make sure I got it right and you were talking about hobnobbing with Prince Malik of Sidra."

"More fishing with every word…"

She splashed him again until he raised his palms. "Yes. Prince Malik. Though we only call him that when he's being particularly pretentious."

Helene smiled again, the real one she'd graced him with before—the one that stopped him in his tracks. "It can be so trying to pal around with royalty."

This time Drake snorted. "You must know from experience, niece and cousin to kings, as you are."

She didn't bother to deny it. "Where else would I come off making a statement like that?"

"Odd sentiment for a royal guard."

Rising to on her back, she let her long body bob in the water while she stared at the stars above. As mesmerized as she appeared by the heavens, he, too, could not seem to take his attention from her. "Not all royalty is created equally," she said. "Zayn, the cousin you mentioned, is as insufferable as you might imagine—intelligent, handsome, excellent at everything—but Mina is different. She was born common, didn't even know she was going to be wed to the king until the day of their wedding."

"A similar story to your own near-engagement," Drake observed, earning a splash from her foot.

"Before becoming queen she was a scientist," she continued.

He was surprised despite himself. "An usual occupation for a future monarch."

Helene smiled, the expression private and protective. "She is an unusual queen."

"You're proud to protect her."

The fact was evident in her voice.

"I am. Zayn is a good king, and my best friend, but Mina… Mina is a gift to the nation. There's only one other person I trust to keep her safe."

Drake quirked an eyebrow. "Somehow I don't imagine that's her husband."

Helene snorted as if the notion was absurd. "Not round-the-clock, no. He's got too many responsibilities for that. He loves her, fiercely, but I meant Moustafa."

"Moustafa?"

"We share guard duty."

"Shared."

Again, she snorted, and added, "*Share.* While

this has been a lovely diversion, in slightly less than six days, I'm going back to work."

Unbothered by her conviction, he offered a small, smug smile. "We'll see."

"We will indeed." Face turning serious, she added, "My father was a bad man, I know it. I've spent my whole life cleaning up the messes he left, only to have new ones swoop in from the sea." Her blue eyes sparkled for him as she spoke and he found himself hypnotized. "I cannot bring your father back or give you your life back, but I am committed to restitution and reparation without breaking my vow."

She made a picture and it eviscerated him—glistening pearly skin, tropical sea-blue eyes, her body barely restrained by straps and swatches of navy fabric of her bikini, unarmed and absolutely unbothered by that fact, and assured in her ability to make the world more just.

Dominic d'Tierrza was dead. His daughter was very much alive. And, having no idea just how close she was to being devoured by the Big Bad Wolf, heedless of just how vulnerable she was to his seduction, she was unwavering in her sweet and brave commitment to right the wrongs of the past. And in that way she made him question himself, question the path he'd chosen, for the first time since Helene had come apart beneath him. Should he continue? Was it right?

His research had revealed her rebellion. It hadn't revealed her innocence. It hadn't revealed the open sensitivity of her responses, or her utter helplessness to them. It hadn't revealed that touching her would fill him with a sense of reverence and honor.

Experience had shown him he had the upper hand when it came to passion. That she was both good and innocent demanded he tread lightly with that power, rather than take advantage of the fact that she came alive at the barest touch. And he would. His revenge didn't demand he lose his honor, just that he not lose his focus, or his heart.

He was old enough to know that once lost, hearts were unrecoverable, and that love, like water, could find a way through even the tightest seams.

A life at sea had taught him that fighting water was the fastest pathway to a watery grave. Like water, no matter the resistance, love got in whether you wanted or not. His father, his mother, his sister, Yancy, Prince Malik—he loved them all. And, for the most part, it was loving all of them that had led to his greatest heartbreaks. What lay between Helene and himself was, and should remain, about triumph and overdue justice, not tender feelings and heartache.

Where love traveled, pain followed, and for the first time in his life, he was ready to celebrate without enduring.

But the waters of love were drawn to the kind of strong physical attraction between them. Whether she realized it or not, he knew the dangers implied when bodies fit together like theirs seemed to.

And while her inexperience was clear, she wasn't clumsy, but merely eager, her energy and attention bright with wonder at what came next. Her enthusiasm alone was a heady aphrodisiac, rousing him to heights he couldn't remember reaching with any other woman.

His balls tightened at the thought, as if he was the one that was brand-new to all of this. And therein was the danger.

Though there was a first time with every new partner, there was something singular to what happened when he and Helene touched.

Either way, wisdom and experience aside, he wasn't the only one with power when they came together…even if she had no idea what to do with it, or even that she had it in the first place.

# CHAPTER SEVEN

HE HADN'T SPOKEN a word since she'd made her statement, but his eyes had communicated a world's worth of data. Heat, anger, passion, desire and more danced across his endless brown gaze.

His arms had fallen out of their habitual crossed position, revealing the massive stretch of his muscled chest. His smooth, deep brown skin, decorated with a surprising arrangement of tattoos, well-placed and balanced on his body, and dusted at his pecs with faint curling hair, cried out to be touched, stroked.

He was more attractive in swim trunks than any man had a right to be. Out of trousers, his legs were thick, as defined and muscled as his chest, and incredibly powerful, even standing at ease in the pool as they were.

His shorts were the perfect length that it

seemed only one man in a million could find—not so long he looked like he might still live with his mother, not so short he seemed like he had something to sell.

As tall as she was, it was rare for a man to make Hel feel small, but standing beside him, craning her neck to remain in the trap of his stare, she was hyperaware of how broad he was in comparison to her own narrow frame.

And if she wanted to keep her vow, if she didn't want to be putty in Drake's hands for the second time this evening, she needed to think of anything else.

Desperate, she reached for something she thought might get him talking, and get that look—intense, possessive and as tangible as a hand at the nape of her neck would have been—off his face. That look that felt like the home that she'd been waiting for her whole life.

"You told me how you got a private island, but how does a poor exile become a foreign-born aristocrat?" she asked. And she wanted to know. It was an incredible feat, particularly following the trauma her father had inflicted.

"Calla was a gift from King Amar for saving his son's life."

"A duchy is a pretty grand gift, even for saving a son. How old were you?" The idea of a king granting a young man a duchy was as medieval to her as Cyrano was thought to be throughout Europe.

Drake gifted her with one of his cocky smiles.

"Twenty-six, and, at the time, Calla was not without its…challenges. King Amar needed a man with naval experience he could trust to take care of the kinds of problems that Calla had, and when I came along, he wasn't going to look a gift horse in the mouth. Even if it was a twenty-six-year-old hothead who'd seemingly come from nothing."

She whistled. "What could you take care of as a young whippersnapper that had stumped a king?" she challenged.

Coming closer, his grin was wide, without a hint of irony. "Pirates."

"I should have known," she groaned.

"Calla had been in the possession of the crown for a number of years following the stripping of titles of the previous duke. By the time I came along, however, they'd turned it into a disaster. Caline was uninhabitable, the bay choked with debris and toxic algae, the arable cropland lying fallow and without irrigation, and everywhere you looked, pirate factions made it impossible for regular people to build lives."

It sounded like a scene from a movie.

"Calla?" Hel asked, astounded. That sounded nothing like the warm and welcoming city she'd experienced.

He nodded. "It took most of the money I earned in the navy, all the way through being an admiral, but once I dealt with the pirates, new residents moved into the area, bringing new commerce along with them. It was only a matter of time before word spread that Calla was once again one of the most highly desirable locations in all of Sidra, and instead of draining my accounts, she began to return on my investment. Tenfold."

Hel smiled. He was proud and he'd earned it. Unlike herself or her cousin or any of the other aristocrats she knew, Drake had built that himself. Not his father or grandfather before him. There was another difference between him and her father. He'd truly created the legacy he was proud of, and in all of that, had not let success corrupt him. He knew hard work and was willing to do it himself—it was a rare trait among the men she'd come of age alongside.

But he clearly didn't need to hear that from her. He had arrogance enough to fill a room. Even one with an open wall to the wide star-filled sky.

Hel shivered, something deep and warm moving inside of her, but she kept her tone light when she finally spoke. "Impressive. A duchy can be a real drain on the pocketbook."

He chuckled, as she'd hoped he would, and the sound warmed her heart. Though she refused to succumb to his charm, she'd make sure she did as right by him as she possibly could.

And she promised to remember the conviction even after they were done luxuriating in the most glorious pool she'd ever been in.

"You never told me why you hate your father so much," he said as if they'd been on the subject.

If he'd meant to throw her off balance with the non sequitur, he was going to be disappointed. She answered without missing a beat. "I did. He was a terrible man, and an actual criminal who terrorized my mother and I."

"Terrorized how?" he persisted.

Looking away, Hel kept it casual. "Yelling, belittling. Hitting before I learned self-defense."

Drake clenched and released his fists, but was even-toned when he asked, "Where was your mother through all of this?"

Instantly protective, Hel's spine straightened. "Being yelled at, belittled and taking the brunt of the hitting until I learned self-defense." Their bond was tied up in more than just the stuff of mothers and daughters.

He pressed, "She didn't keep you safe."

Hel let out a dry, joyless laugh, almost more of a cough than any sound of pleasure. "She couldn't."

"But it still bothers you."

"Not that."

"What?"

When he simply waited for her to respond, she let out an exasperated breath. "She loved him," she finally said.

Drake frowned and she understood his confusion. History was full of powerful men who were bad husbands and evil men yet somehow remained secure in the love of their wives. Though, of course, the d'Tierrza story couldn't be so straightforward. If that had been the case it'd have been a simple thing of rebelling against them both and being done with it. Her relationship with her mother was all the more complicated for the incredible love that bound them together.

"Through it all?" he asked after a long pause, and she was astounded once more by his remarkable perceptiveness. A man didn't come from nothing and make it all the way to the top without being perceptive.

In response, she let out a weary sigh and shook her head, sharing because he had shared so much and, though she'd only now realized it, because she respected him. "No.

Not even love was strong enough to over-come his evil." She hugged her arms around herself, hoping to regain some of the liquid warmth the pool had provided before the chill of telling her deep dark secrets had begun to seep into her bones. "She loved him from the moment she saw him. She was still a teen-ager, and he was actually pursuing my aunt Barbara—she was the prettier one." The aside dripped with bitter hindsight.

"But Barbara ran away with the prince in-stead…"

Hel nodded. That part of the story was well known. Her aunt Barbara had become the queen and her mother the duchess, now dow-ager, of Tierrza.

With a long, slow blink, Hel picked re-turned to the tale. "My mother thought he was so handsome and dashing. He courted Aunt Barbara by the storybook, and my mother ate it all up from the stands—hook, line and sinker. She was only seventeen—young and bright, and too naive to see the obvious rot at his core. They weren't even married yet, the first time he hit her. They'd been engaged for a month. The dress he'd instructed her to wear to an event was damaged the day of, so she changed at the last moment without telling him. She said he gave her a light slap, a little thing really, and that he'd been merely irritated, not enraged. She said at first she was stunned but wrote it off, since it was an important event. He was under a lot of stress. She wrote it off every time after, too. Until I turned sixteen."

After the silence stretched between them, he said, "I would not have thought it possible, but your father was more evil than even I realized."

Helene laughed, the sound not so much joyous as it was the sound of having spent years coming to terms with the fact. "He was." Her father had been an atrocity in so many people's lives, and there would never be enough she could do to make up for it. That kind of ill karma could only be addressed by total annihilation, and the only way she knew how to do that was to ensure that she was the end of the line.

Catching her chin and lifting it, Drake's

warm brown eyes enveloped her, lulled her the same warm water, or a cozy blanket did, safety of a different kind than self-defense provided. "So what happened when you were sixteen?"

His voice was deep and soft, and the warm water of the pool lapped at her legs. The space was intimate, made sacred by the dark confessions she'd already made.

She said quietly, "When I was sixteen, he married me off."

Confusion danced across Drake's gaze. The situation had been scandalous, but very public knowledge. "I read about that," he said carefully.

Hel looked away, wrapping her arms around herself, chilled despite the heated water. "It was later annulled."

She had known her father disdained her before that. After, she'd known it was worse: he didn't care about her at all. He only cared about the name d'Tierrza. She was merely a tool, intentionally created and crafted to enhance the family dynasty.

Drake searched her face, the full force of

his incredible intensity focused on her, and she wished she could create some barrier between them, some way to satisfy him with a simple answer.

But he wasn't easily distracted.

"What happened?" he persisted.

Balling her hands into fists at her sides, Hel took a deep breath and then intentionally released them. "Nothing happened. Because I didn't let it. I had begun studying self-defense and parkour—mainly because he abhorred women with manly pursuits—and if I hadn't…" She met his eyes again, the icy distance in them still the only true defense she had against the indisputable proof of her father's feelings toward her…and the fact it never stopped hurting. "They wanted to force me and wanted to ensure there could be no annulment—the property deal the marriage secured was too important to both families. I was lucky. I escaped my, 'fiancé,' and my mother helped me run away to the academy. We made sure everything was high-profile enough and we made it public enough that there was nothing my father could do, and my fiancé was too embarrassed to have had his butt kicked by the teenage girl he'd tried to force himself on to tell anything but the official story."

An inferno raged in the deep wells of Drake's eyes, but he was utterly controlled, utterly terrifying.

On her behalf.

She had no idea what that meant.

She cleared her throat. "So, yeah. Real bad guy."

"A monster," he agreed.

Hel nodded.

"You're his daughter." He was unflinching without cruelty and it still burned.

Hel's eyelids fluttered closed. When she could speak, she agreed, "Unfortunately."

And there would never be enough she could do to make up for it.

When she opened her eyes, he was watching her with a serious frown, which somehow only emphasized the boy still hidden in his face.

"You are your father's daughter, but you are

not your father, and you are not responsible for his actions," he said.

Her smile was a small and weak thing. "It sure doesn't feel that way."

"Only you can set that burden down."

"I'm strong enough to carry it."

He surprised her when he asked, "But are you strong enough to put it down?" His words were heavy with the weight of the bigger question between them.

She shook her head. "Strength isn't always a good thing."

He frowned, his eyes seeing something far away from the moment they shared. "But it's necessary, nonetheless. There is something poetic in the fact that the strength he gave you would become part of the weapon to destroy him—because whether or not you adopt my plan, you have already defeated him." He shook his head and added quietly, "My father wasn't strong."

Hel frowned. "Your father was heartbroken. No one was more loving or loyal than Uncle Ibrahim." The familiar address rolled off her tongue as smoothly as if it hadn't been nearly thirty years since the last time she'd uttered it.

Looking away, turning to the stars overhead, shining bright through the open viewing wall of the pool room, Drake said, "And he used that as an excuse to break. He left my mother alone, in a strange land, to care for two children in poverty. She had no skills for that…"

And he didn't want to say what it had required of her, because he loved his mother. That much was obvious.

"But you've made up for it now. I imagine she enjoys the good life all the more for having watched her son build it from the ground up…with his own hands."

Instead of the glint of pride that she saw in his eyes whenever he spoke of his accomplishment, Drake closed his eyes with a dry clearing of his throat. "She did."

*Did.* Hel's chest squeezed. "What happened?"

"Breast cancer."

"What?" She'd heard him—of course, she had—but the detail didn't fit with the narrative. How could a woman who had survived such incredible trauma and upheaval, whose life had had all the highs and lows of a long-running television drama, fall to such a quotidian evil as cancer?

Hel would have had an easier time accepting an anvil falling from the sky than the reality that the woman of her memories and Drake's description, one whose light had burned indefatigable, had been snuffed out, betrayed by her own body.

Hel's heart broke for Drake and Nya and Amira, whom she would never reunite with now, no matter how things worked out with her son. The family would have had no skills for the kind of life they found themselves in. But they had endured.

She thought of herself before the rigors of military training and her stubborn will had broken her of the helplessness bred into her by the lap of luxury. What a hard lesson that would have been to learn, and to be forced into it, rather than to have willingly selected it.

They had survived Hel's father, the loss of Ibrahim and poverty. They held, through it all, and long enough for Drake to play Atlas, raising them up through seeming strength of will alone.

Hel would have thought whatever fates existed would have been satisfied with all of that for one family story. But she was apparently destined to be wrong where the fates were concerned.

As if strangely affirming her thinking, Drake said, "My father's love left our family more than half-drowned on a beach. My mother's will brought us back to life. Or, most of us, anyway. And then she died of cancer."

The subtext was clear—whatever had happened to Ibrahim, it was Hel's father who had killed him. Uncle Ibrahim, it seemed, wasn't the type who could come back from being betrayed by someone he loved and trusted so much.

Drake was more like his mother, then— granite-tough and as gorgeous as marble. He was lucky.

Hel's own strength, as he'd noted, came from more tainted sources. She said, "My mother isn't so strong."

The corner of Drake's mouth lifted, a mischievous glint coming to his eye. "I can remember a few times she was strong enough to be downright scary..."

The boyish lightness in his tone shed lines of care from his face, hooking his beauty even deeper into Hel's psyche. She knew that even after this encounter, he would be her standard of male perfection. "I never said she wasn't a mother," she said. "As a mother, she can put the fear of god into your soul. But outside of that, she's...gentle."

"Then she is lucky to have you to protect her."

His words weren't what she had expected to hear, but as they made their way into her heart, something hard and angry cracked and broke, the pieces shaking away to reveal healthy, vibrant emotion beneath.

"Thank you," she said, though it wasn't nearly enough. If she was the type to cry, a tear might have slipped free as she realized, oddly safe and protected by his presence and their isolation, just how hard it had been to carry the shame. And maybe, in this unusual place, she could acknowledge just how much she resented the fact that her mother's weakness meant she had had to bear it alone.

But for this moment, close together and secluded, she could lean into him, the soft smoothness of his skin on hers a sensation far more electrifying than the comfort she might find with her mother, and all the more powerful for it.

Marriage and children might not be her destiny, but if they had been, if she had had the chance to put together an imagined husband, he would have been remarkably like the man she was with now—strong, upright, determined, resilient and committed to justice.

Pulling back, unwilling to lean too hard, to get too used to the support, she was struck by his beauty.

His gaze dropped to her parted lips and her breath caught. The look in his eyes took on an intense focus that hadn't been there a moment before.

He was going to kiss her again, and as her body strained closer to him ever so slightly, she realized she was going to let him again.

She was going to let him, because she *was* strong enough to set it down—her vow, her father, all of it.

She could set it down for Drake.

Their lips met with the shocking electric intensity that was fast becoming an old friend. He was a warm front meeting her cold, the force of their coming together creating a private hurricane of bodies pressed together, his plundering tongue the eye of the storm.

Her long fingers danced across his back and down his arms, freed, uninhibited and empowered to be surprisingly gentle. Everywhere he pulsed warmth and strength—the thrum of blood in his veins beneath his skin, his hands, exploring her body, the growing length of him, separated from her by just the thin fabric of his shorts and her bikini.

Water lapped at their legs, its quiet splashes licking up only to drip down her inner thighs as the mingled sound of their heavy breathing echoed and swirled throughout the pool room like steam in a sauna.

His roughened sailor's palms came to rest at her lower rib cage before caressing her in an upward motion, his thumbs brushing under and along the outer edges of her breasts, exposed on either side of her bikini top. Her skin tightened at the contact, shivers trailing their way outward from her spine to the tips of her extremities, chasing the breath out of her lungs as if at the end of breath lurked bliss. Her sigh was pressure released in pleasure, escaping her swollen lips to weave them together before she even recognized the sound as her own.

He growled in response, the sound a rumble originating somewhere near where their hips ground against each other before it vibrated up through his torso to become pure possession in his kiss.

She moaned into him, giving him more of her weight, more of her need, more of her.

He answered by running his hand down her side to catch her thigh, lifting it in a smooth motion, bringing them even closer, core to nuclear core. And still, it wasn't enough. She still wanted more.

Greed was a new experience.

When resources were infinite, there was

no want or lack to breed greed. But here, between them, she met limits for the first time—a limit in how close she could press, a limit in how she could assuage the growing chasm inside that cried out for more even after being given more than it had ever been given before, a limit in her ability to join with him, as if the brand-new concept the primitive voice inside whispered to her was not only possible, but also imperative. They could become one, it promised. If she was brave enough, their essence could unify, creating a new entity, greater than the sum of their perfectly suited parts.

It was a fascinating lure. Truly tempting, in a way none of the tepid stolen kisses of her past had been. It wasn't possible to be a beautiful, rich, female royal without having had her fair share of unwanted advances. Before she'd become strong enough to fend them off in other ways, she'd learned that the best response was simply to reveal to the absolute chill of disinterest their efforts inspired in her. But the truth was, until Drake, she had never been tempted.

His kisses made her forget herself, lose her sense of time and place. There was no upper hand under the command of his lips.

And she couldn't get enough.

Neither, it seemed, could he. With another growl, this one dogged by frustrated need, he scooped up her other thigh, unbalancing her as he took her weight easily, holding her body—hot, slick and wet—tight against his… all without breaking his kiss.

He was strong. Stronger than she was, she noted, though she usually didn't think in terms like that. Strength was nothing against determination—unless that strength was a volcano rising from the sea, threatening to engulf her in its molten waves. He was overwhelming, and she realized she wanted to be overwhelmed, but only by him.

Without breaking the kiss, he carried her to the edge of the warm pool, placing her there gently, as if she was something delicate and fragile, rather than the same woman he'd sparred with only yesterday morning.

Standing between her parted thighs, he brought his hands up to cup her jaw, his touch reverent as he tilted her face up toward his to plunder the depths of her mouth further. And then his fingers were in her hair, massaging her scalp as his lips made mush of her mind.

Everything in her strained toward him, reaching for that elusive union her body insisted was their ultimate destination. Her breasts ached, longing for what she didn't know, while everywhere her skin flushed and burned.

His lips followed his hands, tracing her jawline to find her earlobe, where he bit her softly before whispering something long and lovely in Sidran. And then all the air, and her wits, rushed out of her at the same time, every ounce of her focus zeroed in on the point where his thumbs pressed against her aching nipples.

Blue triangles of swimsuit separated them, but she felt the contact as acutely as if she had been nude, each rosy peak exposed beneath the dark sky.

And then he was rolling the hard pearls between his thumb and forefinger, his palms joining in the sensual explosion, cupping and lifting her breasts, and she was arching her back, pressing herself farther into his hands.

Snaking an arm around her waist to hold her, he kissed down her neck, pillaging the ivory column all the way, his free arm working its way behind her back and pulling the string that held her top in place.

He made quick work of the string around her neck, tossing the top to the side as he pulled back to feast on the sight of her bare breasts. The look in his eyes said he was ravenous for a sustenance only she could provide. In that instant, she felt what it was to be a font—a source of life, beauty and wonder—rather than an embattled soldier with grim purpose.

It felt like earning wings.

His hot mouth locked around the needy peak of her nipple and she soared, the sensation breaking free in the form of his name on her lips, the syllable a drawn-out cry of pleasure. Her legs squeezed around his waist of their own volition, the movement a subconscious flirtation, drawing him nearer to the untapped power source at her core.

Her movement set off a tremor of reaction through his body that she felt deep within her own. She marveled that she had the ability to make this incredible man shake. The thought went straight to her head, light and bubbly even as it was tremendous, like standing on the edge of a skyscraper.

Her breath came in shallow pants as he devoured her, switching to the other breast only when he'd completely ravished the first, his free hand quickly coming to replace the spot where his mouth had been.

She was putty in his hands, his to play with and mold, pliable and unguarded in a way she hadn't been since long before the days they'd chased each other through the flowers as children.

He didn't waste the opportunity.

His tongue traced lines of fire around her breasts, driving her mad in a tempest of temperature and taste and tightening. His beard and teeth gave an edge to every sensation, the combination of sandpaper and silk keeping her spinning.

And then he said her name.

It was more of a breath than even a whisper, but it shot through her, lacy and lithesome as it was, rolling off his tongue with hushed reverence.

"Helene."

No one called her that. Hel. D'Tierrza. Duke. Captain. Not even her mother, who preferred the term *daughter* most of the time.

Hel had always hated *Helene*, fussy and formal, perfect and composed—everything she stood in opposition of.

Until now. The moment he said it, his tone worshipful, his lips soft against her skin as he spoke, she was transformed.

*Helene* had the power to bring this god of the sea to his knees. It was the knowledge, from wherever it arose, that he could weather her most powerful storms, and be strong, steady and, most of all, kind.

Rock-hard and warm beneath her hands, he was living, throbbing, ready proof that maybe she was wrong, that maybe, just maybe, incredible strength could come without cruelty.

And whether it was due to that seismic realization or the onslaught of his sensual attack, her body began to tremble. What had begun as faint tremors grew into stronger, more insistent rolling waves, threatening to carry her out to sea, relentless in their increasing strength as her power to resist waned.

"Show me," he demanded, his voice guttural, all the more commanding for playing her like a maestro at his instrument. "Show me how you fall apart."

She wanted to fight. She wasn't the kind of woman who complied easily—she was famous for it—and yet her body strained toward his, the gnawing hunger coalescing where she shamelessly pressed against him.

Yet still she resisted.

She might retreat, but she didn't surrender.

"Do it now," he said, and he took one nipple in his mouth at the same instant as he pinched the other and she exploded into a brand-new galaxy—herself, her energy, her very life bursting into a vast collection of stars, planets and memories, spread out before her for an endless second.

His palm scraped lightly down the long plane of her belly, branding her as his as surely as a cattleman's mark. Then the tips of his long fingers slipping beneath the top edge of her swimsuit and stopped.

He pulled back, commanding her gaze. He was beautiful—his brown eyes burning in low light, his incredible physique harnessed and focused entirely on her, his glorious erection obvious—and he was absolutely not going any further without her signal.

And even though none of it was for her, not marriage, and certainly not children, just for tonight, in this magical place so far from her regular life, she wanted to pretend it was. Disheveled and thoroughly taken, her lips swollen and sensitive, her deepest core throbbing and hungry, aching, craving and insistent that there was more despite his thorough gorging, she nodded.

# CHAPTER EIGHT

SLIDING HER BLUE bikini down revealed the trim triangle of white-blond curls, a treasure he was desperate to cup, hold, slide his finger along the seam of and slip inside… Muscles straining, he refrained. Instead, he brought his fingertip back up to the center point between her eyebrows and trailed down, skin lightly touching skin, all the way down, over her chin, down her neck, between her breasts, past her belly button, only to stop at the beginning of that triangle. She sucked in her breath on a soft hiss, her skin tightening, back arching. Her skin was soft and sensitive for a woman who made a living of being hard.

Moonbeams streaming in through the sky-view wall lit and outlined her perfection—her nipples, dusky rose and proud, her breasts, soft and pliant, each one his perfect handful, her waist, slender and long, the rounded swell of her hips and muscular curvature of her backside, each line an artist's, emphasizing her form with shadow and highlight.

Rock-hard and throbbing, the tip of his manhood was damp in anticipation of her, as if it knew this was her first time, knew that even though he would take care of her, that he would ensure she was as wet the ocean floor before he entered her, that she would need all of that and more to ease his entry.

He was a lot to take for the first time, but he had no doubt she could handle him—all of him—like a custom-made sheath. A captain learned to trust his instincts, and his instincts were screaming that he had found his Penelope. But unlike famous Odysseus, he would not ask her to put her life on hold. He would set her free.

But not until he'd heard her beg. If she was going to make his dreams come true, he was going to blow her mind.

While she still shook, he took her further under his command, gripping her hips on either side, strong fingers digging into the taut flesh. Adjusting her position, he sat her on the edge of the pool and spread her legs, an open buffet for his feast.

Languorous and love-drunk, she was unprepared for the onslaught. He attacked directly, no longer content to resist the siren song of her scent.

She tasted like citrus, snapping him back to the bright bergamot that infused the private courtyard air outside his childhood bedroom in Andros, a sensory pleasure long-lost—she tasted like home. Even when he'd tasted her for the first time, the knowledge hadn't surprised him, as if some part of him had known the moment he'd laid eyes on her, watching her argue with the ghost of her father.

He could have told her there was no use arguing with that man.

But then he wouldn't have her here, slick and hot and sumptuous.

She screamed his name as his tongue teased the crease at her core.

Her fingers found his shoulders, her hands strong and capable, and she held onto him like a life raft when, in fact, he was the storm.

He couldn't remember ever being this hard, this eager, this close to the edge from little more than the sound of her pleasure and a taste.

Of course, he couldn't remember a taste quite like her before, either. And as she bulldozed the competition in his record book, he was taken aback at what was happening to him. She was mesmerizing him, luring him into a dazed stupor with every passing and savored second he spent with his hands on her, his mouth on her…and if he went further, if he steered them into a union, as was his undeniable plan, she would wreck him.

What was happening between them, what blossomed, was as far from the careless encounters of a sailor on leave as a lake from the ocean. This was the stuff of forever, and deeper connection, and baring real emotions. Everything paled in comparison to Hel because he had never felt this for another woman. Their bodies told him what their battle-weary hearts resisted: this was the stuff of love.

It was too late to change course now, though.

Sometimes the only way out of a storm was through it.

He was ready for the tempest when she came apart the second time, lapping her up like a fool in the rain. Her thighs clenched around his head and he smiled against her, glorying in each and every one of her unintentional reactions, each reflexive tightening and release, each pulsing wave that carried her away with as much surprise as joy.

She would carry this memory of him with her forever. He'd make sure it was unforgettable.

He held her there, helpless to both his attack and her pleasure, until her hips relaxed in his hands and the pulses of her climax slowed, her breathing jagged and airy.

Again, he knew she thought she was done, wrung out. It was written in the boneless fall of her body, the dazed glimmer in her eyes.

Humming a long "mmmmm" against her, he began to trail kisses upward again, over her stomach, before stopping to shower her breasts with more attention. In no time at all, her soft sighs grew heavier, elongated and interspersed with drawn-out pauses, moments of time standing still.

While he kissed the plump underside of her breasts, his hand returned south, finding the heat of her core. Fingers once again playing along her entrance, his thumb found the little bud at the top that held the key to it all and pressed with gentle firmness, before beginning the alternating dance of pressure and release that would push her over the edge yet again.

If anything, she was more responsive. And why should he be surprised? Her body was a well-honed machine—of course, she responded to practice like a master. She was a true wonder.

He slipped one long finger inside as she moaned and her inner muscles clenched around him so hard he groaned, sweat beading on his forehead. It was absurd—she couldn't be this tight and hot and not kill him. Her body was a vise around his finger, so snug the thought even flitted across his own mind. Would he fit?

He had always laughed the concern away

in the past, as confident in the engineering of nature as he was in his endowment, but now, when it mattered more than it ever had, he doubted.

Would she be ready? Could she take him? He didn't want to hurt her.

He slipped another finger in, stilling both digits to allow her time to adjust and stretch.

A tremor radiated from her center outward and he shuddered, unsure if he would make it for the first time in his life. His control had been ironclad the night three older friends had taken him to a house of ill repute to make a man of him.

Tonight, it threatened to break with each silken compression.

Would he survive it?

Whatever the answer, the time was at hand. Knowing throbbed in him as hard and hot as he was.

Rising over her, he was filled with an unfamiliar wave of possession. Eyes glittering, she stared up at him, unflinching and hungry despite having been sated time and again. She belonged to him and no one else.

She would let him in, and him alone. He could offer her a part of himself and never fear betrayal.

Without words, her body whispered the most tempting lure of all. *You can trust me*, it promised, and the incredible thing was, he believed he could.

The revelation was heady and powerful.

Reaching an arm between them, he gripped himself, already cloudy with his excitement. Then he ran his sensitive head along the same hot seam that his fingers had traced earlier, torturing them both with the electric waves each movement set off.

Breath catching, her fingers squeezed into his shoulders, when he paused at her entrance, pressing just slightly, holding there, breath, time, life itself on pause for the space of a heartbeat, before continuing the sweet agony of the caress.

She whimpered beneath him, hips lifting unconsciously inviting him deeper.

Where the strength came from, he could not say, but he held fast.

She pressed against him, body rooting for

the next level of pleasure she sought if her mind didn't yet know what it wanted and needed.

Maintaining the game was excruciating. He knew he could plunge into her at any moment and she would scream in relief, the fullness her body instinctively knew it craved achieved, but he did not.

Her sighs and moans became puffs of frustration and her eyes flew open, irritation as clear as the blue in her gaze. Faint pink danced across her cheeks, flushed and glowing as she was, and it was all he could do to hold the line.

His shaft virtually wept for release, but he denied them.

She shifted her hips, opening wider, giving him greater access. He groaned, muscles taut and screaming, body screaming, throbbing, screaming, but continued to tease.

Another noise of frustration and then the word he had been waiting for, breathlessly uttered and slipping between her plump lips.

"Please."

It was a whole sentence when she said it.

She needed something from him, didn't know what it was, but trusted him to interpret her impassioned plea and give it to her.

"Please, Drake," she said again, his name an intoxicating addition.

And he could hold back no longer.

He plunged into her in one stroke, using all his strength to hold still, and he strained under the assault of sensations. Heat, grip, slick and pulsing. Fully sheathed, her body held him like a vise. They stayed like that, still joined, while the veins in his neck bulged. She might kill him, but he would die happy.

And then she began to stir and it was only iron will that stopped him from embarrassing himself.

Tentative at first, soon she was exploring the feel of him with her characteristic boldness. And when he knew he could take no more, he took charge, setting a slowly building rhythm. He knew the instant the smooth friction snared her attention, baiting her down the path of falling part yet again.

When another hot wet wave engulfed him, he knew she was close. Close enough to increase his pace, diving and driving her harder and deeper, her increasing moans telling him everything he needed to know about her enjoyment. And when even that wasn't enough, when he had to push harder, deeper, she kept pace without lagging, her energy more than enough to match him, her strength promising him he couldn't break her.

His name was her last word, called out like a dying woman before her body tightening stole the very breath from him, before she broke into a thousand searing convulsions. The realization that would be burned into his soul from this moment forward was his last coherent before he was tossed to sea himself, pounding to the very depths of her before breaking into a million little pieces.

He came to with his arm wrapped around her, holding her upright in the curve of his arm, her legs dangling in the pool.

She radiated the contentment they both felt, bodies joined and humming in tune, the physical evidence of the way things had changed.

Because things had changed.

He was unwilling to look at the most profoundly intimate sexual encounter he'd ever had and pretend otherwise.

His mother's words, her ever-optimistic mantra, whispered in the back of his mind. *You never know what flowers the manure will turn up.*

His arrangement with Helene might not have grown from love, but the potential for it was there. That much was as clear as the blue of her eyes. That he could love, not merely tolerate, the daughter of Dominic d'Tierrza was a testament to the power of the emotion, the idea so foreign that the possibility had never once occurred to him all of his plotting—not even after seeing her and realizing the task might not be so onerous as he'd once imagined. Only now.

It was a delicious if unexpected icing on the cake he'd finally gotten a slice of—because if her actions were any indication, and this matter was one in which action was as good as word, she had agreed to be his accomplice, his partner in justice. Even when his mind and body were tempted to float away in favor of examining emotions other than triumph, reticent emotions that lurked beneath the surface, entirely unconcerned with obsession and revenge, and all the more powerful for it.

Those emotions were best left for times after they'd worked through their shared business.

Her vow had been thoroughly burned to ashes.

His children, his name, would replace d'Tierrza on the map.

That victory had come wrapped up in the most phenomenal package he'd ever had the pleasure of opening, was more than a cherry on top.

If they had not already achieved his ultimate goal of seating his children on the d'Tierrza throne, it would certainly be a pleasure to try again. And again.

The incredible had occurred: he'd gotten his cake and got to eat it, too. He'd turned tragedy into triumph so monumental that he was on the verge of pinching himself. He couldn't stop the smile that stretched wide as he pulled her close and nuzzled his face in her hair, drawing in the fresh scent of her, before shifting her gently. Her noise of protest had him wincing, tightness squeezing his chest as he pulled back. He'd been lost in thought when he needed to see to her comfort.

"It's time to get you out of this pool. I'm sure you're wrinkled all over by now."

She groaned, the sound a tremor quaking through her body. He felt it like a knife edge along the oversensitive line where they were still connected. He slid out of her slowly, careful to go easy, knowing she'd be sore nonetheless.

More groaning came from her, but he could tell it was merely on principle now. He was surprised to find it...cute.

For the briefest second, he wondered if she was some kind of sleeper agent, the ultimate coup de grâce of Dominic d'Tierrza's grand evil schemes, even while he knew it wasn't possible.

A move like that would have required that

he understand things like love, and need, and the cruel choices of the heart.

To the world's great fortune, Dominic had not been aware of exquisite agonies of the warmer emotions. If he had realized love could burn like fire, he would have seen his daughter as a weapon, instead of merely a pawn. That he had done even that, and that it was only her own ingenuity that had kept her safe from his machinations, was repulsive enough.

But as childhood images of her flashed through his mind, he wondered if perhaps Dominic had understood more about his daughter's potential than he'd ever let on.

In his memory, it was as if she had always been there, a constant companion at his side, carried around to protect and encourage and goad and draw smiles from, rather than a woman with whom he'd only recently become reacquainted.

He gave his head a shake to free it from the cobwebs of melodrama. It was time to get out of the pool and away from his gorgeous linchpin.

But first he drew her closer again.

She softened against him, her eyes closing on an exhale.

Just like that, they fit together—as naturally as if they had been made to comfort one another.

They stood together in the pool without words as the sun made its debut, its light dancing across the black waves of the sea, bursting free to bring blue to the sky.

Helene opened her eyes in the growing light, the pool room sparkling, and he watched the realization dawn on her that the room's nighttime performance had been mere sleepwalking, that it truly woke with the dawn, its bright white walls near blinding, its mosaics glittering like paintings rendered with multifaceted gemstones. The room itself was a treasure chest, the water of the pool crystalline turquoise, the beautiful cushions of fabrics and pillows even more stunning by day.

"Are you hungry?" he asked, enjoying the irritation that flickered across her face at being asked such a mundane question after all they had shared.

"You're always trying to feed me," she grumbled.

"You're too skinny," he insisted, to her outrage.

She crossed her arms in front of her chest.

"On a normal day, I eat three thousand calories!" she said.

"So you say," he said, shrugging. "Your frame speaks for itself, however."

Her eyes narrowed, glittering in the light as jewel-toned as the mosaics beneath their feet.

Her statement was ruined, however, when Hel's stomach grumbled.

Squinting in the ever-brightening room, he turned a grin her direction and said, "You're hungry. And tired, I'm sure, after our little adventures. We'll eat, rest and then we'll return to Cyrano to destroy your father's legacy."

From the pool room, it looked as if the sun had bleached out every color except for blue on the island, the palm fronds mostly silhouetted against the sand and sea.

She nodded, eyes wide blue orbs in her moon-pale face reflecting the impossible blue of the sea in the distance, as well as the topaz-clear waters of the pool. Her cheeks had pinkened again, making her look like a porcelain doll...but he knew she was far from fragile.

Lifting himself from the water, he wrapped a towel around his waist before reaching out a hand to assist her.

Taking it, she followed his lead, wrapping her towel to hang low around her hips, and he shook his head, his smile growing. Most women would have covered their whole bodies.

Helene wasn't most women.

He walked them out of the room, toward the kitchen.

The compound on Yancy Grove was impressive, considering its foundations were historic, if not ancient—he didn't know for certain because accurate structural dating of the original foundations was less important than privacy.

Over the years he had improved the existing ruins, maintaining structural integrity wherever he could, and made sure that every element of new architecture blended stylistically with what remained.

The result was like traveling back to the times of the great African kings. Wide walkways lined with fragrant blooming vines created the boundaries for smoothly tiled hallways. Cleverly placed arched cutouts in the walls encouraged the sea air to dance through the buildings, cooling as they went, as well as ensuring there wasn't a poor view to be had. The complex of buildings was loosely rectangular, arranged around a central courtyard with a massive, three-tiered fountain in its center. The fountain was classic with simple flowing lines and flourishes rather than ornate carvings with waterspouts. Palm trees and flowering shrubs grew wherever there was space, giving everything a feeling of overgrowing paradise, newly discovered, like the day they'd stumbled upon it so desperately.

Flat-roofed buildings had staggered heights, architecturally anchored by the domed roofs of each corner building, which created spaces for rooftop dining, as well as a rooftop shower and soaking pool.

Between the pool room and roofs, he could spend every moment in the open air should he want to, just like his days at sea, as if the island itself was his ship.

There was no retiring from the sea.

He led Helene through the perfumed corridors between the pool room, into the smaller of the kitchen and dining rooms. Yancy Grove was structured so that it could accommodate his whole crew and their immediate families should the need arise, but it was also comfortable to reside in alone. After all, that was how he spent most of his time on the island.

In the kitchen, he indicated that she should take a seat at the counter-island bar chair, while he prepared them a meal, the significance of what had just transpired heavy and unspoken between them.

"You cook?"

He lifted an eyebrow. "I like to eat."

She grinned. "So do I, and I don't know the difference between a sauté pan and a boiling pot."

"At the very least you know what you don't know," he said dryly.

She laughed, watching avidly as he sprinkled seasonings. "What are we having?"

"Lightly seared ahi steaks."

"Sounds delicious. You don't have staff here?"

Eyeing her, he said, "Your pampered lifestyle is showing, princess."

Hel made a rude gesture with her hand in response. "I don't need staff. I just expected you would have them."

"And why is that?"

It was Hel's turn to be dry. "You're a double duke."

Her words landed like cold darts. She was right, though he had never truly thought of himself as Duke Andros. That had been his father most of the time and his stolen birthright otherwise.

Instead of the elation he had felt earlier, the knowledge came with a strange sense of emptiness. What was there now that he had achieved his greatest dream?

But to Helene, he said, "I started out as a humble sailor."

Helene rolled her eyes. "Then became an admiral and a duke."

He shook his head, grin flashing. "No. I was a duke before I was an admiral."

"And impossible even before that," she retorted.

Still grinning, he gave her a little salute before taking the platter of steaks out to the grill. Minutes later he returned to the kitchen, seared ahi ready to serve.

He set the table for the two of them easily, laying out island-grown dates and figs, as well as fresh goat cheese, bread and olives, brought from the mainland by his staff during their once-weekly trips.

He finally answered her question as she joined him in the bright sky-lit breakfast nook. "I don't keep regular staff here because I like the privacy. I only have guests when I want them."

But he found he didn't mind sharing the space with Helene.

He had been observing her from the moment he'd seen her in the d'Tierrza courtyard, catching the unguarded moments between her forced nonchalance when her expression was fierce, earnest and so transparent he could read her thoughts like a marquee.

That this woman could be the product of Dominic d'Tierzza was unbelievable.

An entire world had gone up against Dominic d'Tierrza, and as far as Drake could tell, the only one who had walked out even remotely whole was the woman eating at his side. As incredible as it was, and despite the fact that he would have carried out his plans regardless of who she was, respect and affection for her had taken root in their short time together. He hadn't intended or thought it even possible, but, beyond their incredible sex, he truly liked her.

Or maybe plotting revenge for thirty years had finally pushed him over the edge.

After breakfast, they agreed to rest, though he wasn't sure how much sleep he would be getting.

Hours spent with Helene were akin to plugging in to a live wire. He was electrified.

He showed her a set of rooms she could use, equipped with their own bathroom and shower, and left her there while he found a change of clothes for her in the supplies closet.

After laying them on the bed, he left the room to take his own shower and rest.

As energizing as her company was, he ultimately fell asleep quickly. Being in the military for so long had taught him to take advantage of opportunities to sleep when he could.

Hours later, he woke, fully alert the moment his eyes opened, another holdover from a career in the service. He was hyperaware of the absence of Helene.

He found her, equally alert, when he rapped on her door. She looked rested, though he wasn't certain how he could tell, having never observed her looking tired.

He had never met another woman who embodied the word *indefatigable* so well, something he appreciated as buoyant as he was feeling.

"How did you sleep?" he asked, smile wide

and warm. He was eager to begin planning the next stage now that he had secured her cooperation, but he had the sense not to start when she'd only just woken up.

Seeing her again, though, after their time in the pool, had his blood thrilling again, his pulse as jumpy and eager as a little boy with a big present.

Impossibly, she was even more beautiful. They had slept much of the day, which was to be expected after almost sixty hours of near constant activity. It was past the normal dinner hour, but still bright enough outside that he considered a late dinner alfresco. And after that, they could christen another pool room.

He loved that she was so at ease in the water.

Her smile was coral magic. "Wonderfully, thank you."

His mouth quirked up at those impeccable manners. Blue-blooded-ness really was her default, for all that she was a soldier.

"Are you hungry?"

"Trying to feed me yet again?" She quirked up an eyebrow.

"Can I help it if I was raised right?"

She smiled and for an instant he simply let himself appreciate the way the smile warmed him. He was driven, determined and unstoppable. It was easy to forget he was also a man. A man who wanted to hold his woman, for just a breath, before they got back to work.

"I'm not hungry, but I would like a walk on the beach," she said.

"Then a-walking we will go. There are spare sandals where the slippers were." He offered her his arm and she smiled at him, cheeks tinged with pink, and took it.

They walked together, arm in arm, while he marveled at the lightness between them. She was a royal guard, a consummate professional, and he was a retired admiral turned privateer specializing in hunting down traffickers, and together, they were in the business of revenge, and yet there was a lightness to being around Helene…as if alongside work, there could be play.

"Do I need sandals on a deserted island?" she asked, a light in her eyes.

He shook his head. "You have something against footwear?"

She laughed, stretching her arms wide. "I don't like being hemmed in. I told you. It's the barefoot-and-free-seafaring life for me now."

He snorted. "More like the barefoot-with-babies life for you now. At least temporarily."

Laughing, she said, "Well, not right away! I've got to get back to work eventually, and now that I've broken the seal, there's so much to explore before babies…"

He stopped, still smiling. "There's no rule that says we have to stop exploring when you're pregnant. But we should begin right away if we want the best chances. The process of marriage and unifying titles is lengthy and should be begun immediately, as well. It's hitting the ground running and a lot all at once, but in the long run, it's just two to three years…"

Stopping beside him, Hel frowned, a sense of warning, like a frigid gust, blowing through the languorous tingles that had been pulsing in her body ever since the pool room. "I can't get pregnant now," she said. "It's not the right time with my job."

He smiled. "While we both know you're far from decrepit, at your age, it's best we don't waste time."

Hel snorted, "Calling me old now? Hardly. I'm in fantastic shape. And we certainly have options if that traditional way didn't work out." She blushed, her body still tender and alive with doing things the traditional way. "Kids and marriage will need to wait, if only temporarily," she assured him with a grin, then added, "but in the meantime, we can keep practicing..."

But the flirty grin she expected didn't flash across his face. Instead, his eyebrows came together, shadowing his eyes, bringing turbulence to his expression. "How long?" he asked, his voice rough and salty, older than she'd ever heard it.

Taking a step back, she wrapped her arms around herself. She was chilled, whereas before she'd felt loose and easy. "I don't know. A year, maybe two? It's not long to wait."

"I could say the same to you and science would be on my side," he said, crossing his arms in front of his chest.

A strange pressure filled her lungs, making her breath come thick and heavy.

"It's just not a good time. There is the royal wedding, and my mother will expect a full wedding before we start announcing grandchildren."

"We'll elope," he said, as if that made everything easy.

Hel's head began to throb, the sensation of tightening, an ever-intensifying squeezing spreading throughout her whole body, familiar for all that she couldn't place it.

"My mother will want a wedding."

He scoffed. "It's not your mother's nuptials. What she wants is irrelevant."

And then Hel knew. She knew where she'd felt this before. She knew why she had the urge to fight—to kick and scream and do exactly the opposite of what he wanted from her. His words were an echo of her father.

"I want a wedding. I want to wait until the timing is better before *I* have children. That means after the royal wedding, and after our wedding, and maybe even after a honeymoon," Hel retorted, her hands coming to rest on her hips as her temperature kicked up with each word, despite the cool sea breezes. "You've asked me for my entire life, to abandon my own quest for justice, to have your children, and I have, in a matter of days, which is a remarkably quick turn of fashion, I'd say. I'm just asking you for a year, at most, two. I gave you my word."

"In my experience, the word of a d'Tierrza isn't worth a lot."

She lifted an eyebrow, danger slipping into her voice. "I am not my father. You either trust me or you don't."

His eyes narrowed, equal ferocity coming to his expression. "I can't say that I think much of your conviction, based on my personal experience. In fact, in my experience, you've only been able to hold out, for what was it you mentioned? A matter of days."

The color drained from her face. "Excuse me?" she asked, her head cocked at a stiff angle, her body rigid with the pain each successive word launched.

She had been so mature. So reasonable about the whole thing. She had been flexible and open, willing to alter her course in the name of honor.

She made choices with her eyes open, knowing what and why he wanted. So why did his words feel like darts? Why did she feel such a deep aching in the center of her chest?

It couldn't simply be sex, could it? Yes, he had been her first and she knew how easy it was to entangle sex with emotion, but they were both adults. She was mature enough to realize the two didn't automatically go hand in hand.

So why did it hurt when he threw what she'd given him at her like that? Why did it hurt, that he dictated careless of her needs, wants and desires? Why did she feel like a child all over again, simultaneously wanting to strike and to please him? Why did she feel like ten times a fool at the same time, blithely walking into her mother's fate—that of the tragic, foolish and abused woman—when she'd sworn to herself it would never be hers?

"I'm just saying the evidence of your ability to keep your word is sadly lacking." His words were flat. Dismissive. Distinctly unimpressed.

The rising heat in her body dissipated like a popped balloon.

He had gone past anger.

Lust and longing would not make a pawn or a slave out of her—she wouldn't allow it. She had been caught up, ensnared and foolish enough to falter once, but never again. And it started immediately. She would never let a man dictate to her, no matter what she'd given him. Never.

She stood still, her body's readying itself reminiscent of the surf being pulled out to sea before a tsunami. It was quiet, eerie, all wrong, though it would have been hard to immediately pinpoint why. "Take me home. Immediately."

For a moment he just stared. She couldn't be serious. She had broken her vow. She had agreed to his plan. She was dedicated and honorable. She wasn't backing out now. "What? That's absurd."

"Take. Me. Home. Now. I say no and it's over."

His ears roared like the inside of a conch shell. This was not happening. She'd already given up her vow. She couldn't go back now. They'd gone too far. The roaring took on a tunneling quality. "Did it occur to you," he said, proud of how steady and even he kept his voice, "that it might already be too late?"

Horror filled her eyes, transforming into two bottomless pits of sapphire, and the expression was a knife in his gut. "The odds of human conception in any given encounter are rather low, so while, yes, it occurred to me, I was not so naive as to jump to that conclusion."

"I wouldn't be so quick to assume averages would apply to the two of us," he said, the words tasting bitter on his tongue. She, like everything else in her hands, became a weapon.

She rolled her eyes. "Right. I might be pregnant because the big bad Sea Wolf looked at me. That's a pretty high opinion you have of yourself. But why should I be surprised?"

The flare of his temper was as unwelcome as the realization that he wasn't entirely in control—of himself or the situation.

It was a novel experience.

"What's that supposed to mean?" he asked, pleased with his low and even tone.

Anger danced in her eyes. "Why should I be surprised that a man like you thinks he's somehow above everyone around him, that the air he breathes is so rarified that it gives him the right to make decisions for everyone around him?"

His eyes narrowed, his glare warning her to quit while she was ahead.

She didn't back down. "Why should I be surprised when I have known that man my whole life?"

He didn't explode, though his anger at being compared to her father by her was as deep and thick as the molten lava waiting to burst forth from below the earth.

With the words out, unable to be taken back,

she eyed him warily with an expression that he would have said was tinged with sadness had it graced any face other than hers. She burned too hot for something so cold and wet as regret.

He returned her regard from a remove, a distance that was entirely invisible separating them, and separating him from what he said.

"He'd be dead and gone if you didn't work so hard to keep his memory alive, Helene. He died years ago and yet you talk to him like he's alive. In fact, Helene, he is. You keep him alive with every breath you take. You look in the mirror and deep in your eyes, you know the person who looks back is him, and no matter what you do to offset his evil in the world it won't matter because as long as you exist to do battle with him, he lives." And if his words applied to himself, too, it didn't matter, because he had scored his point.

Pain lanced her expression, but the tears that glistened in her eyes did not fall. Instead, she jutted out her chin at a stubborn angle and he was instantly sent back, the image of her now superimposed over the dusty memories his mind had stored of her from when they'd been children together.

Coltish even as a young child, Helene, he recalled, had been nonstop energy from sunup to sundown, absolutely determined to keep up with her older playmate. Absolutely determined that no one—certainly not a twelve-year-old boy—would dominate her.

He felt an undeniable déjà vu comparing his images of the child Helene to the woman who stood before him.

"I said I'd give you seven days, but I've made my mind up already. I will not be a part of your plot. I will not be your pawn. I promised myself on the steps of the academy that I would never let a man like my father control me, ever again. I meant it. Not him, and certainly not you. Take me back to Cyrano. I want to go home now."

His eyes blazed rage at her, impotent as it was, as the plan he'd waited thirty years for went up in flames, laced with an even sharper pain, an underlying and relentless acid ache that started in his chest and radiated outward, as if his heart was being slowly eaten alive.

And it was worse since there had been more than mere revenge between them, because, whether she knew it or not, the potential for something real existed between them.

Like a child with no thought to the devastation of her words, she carelessly compared him to his greatest nemesis while simultaneously tearing at the new, dangerous and delicate thing that beat in his chest, the thing that wanted to please her.

He smiled, though the expression felt as dry and brittle as a barking cough. "Certainly," he said. He kept his voice firm and cool, though for the life of him, he could not recall words cutting his mouth so sharply on the way out.

He had trusted her. Trusted her to keep her word, to go along with his crazy idea, and the sting he felt at her betrayal was stronger than anything he'd felt since discovering his father's suicide or his mother's cancer, or even what he'd felt as he held Yancy as he'd died. When she'd given herself to him, she'd agreed, she'd taken his hand and he'd dared to hope.

She had given him her body, and he'd mistaken it for something more, trusting the breaking of her vow to speak for her. Replaying the events, it was obvious trusting was where he had gone wrong. Who knew better than he that even the most reliable constants could abandon you when you most needed them?

He didn't know what he was doing anymore. That much was clear. He couldn't trust people—not with his thoughts, not with his emotions and certainly not with his hopes and dreams. Trust was a luxury of the privileged, and even then, only few.

But he would not take back his words. He'd meant what he said when he told her he didn't force women. When one made it a policy to only speak the truth, there was nothing to ever take back.

Once again he looked out over the Mediterranean, squinting against the bright sun shining on the bright white sand and bright cerulean sea, the wheels of his crystalline mind turning.

Following the shoreline, observing the palm

trees swaying gently in the breeze that were rooted atop small grassy dunes dotting the swaths of almost antiseptically white sand, it occurred to him that she might be right.

Perhaps he was like her father, as ravenously hungry and driven by greed. He had everything and more that a hard-scrapping poor boy could dream of, and he had the strength and resilience he would have been denied had the silver spoon he was born with not been ripped from his mouth.

Recognizing it did nothing to soothe the roar inside, but it underscored Helene's point.

He was used to the abyss, had grown comfortable with its unceasing demand for nothing less than the total annihilation of his enemies.

It wasn't her black hole to bear. Was even, his conscience warned as it threaded its way to the surface of his mind to remind him, wrong to ask of her.

To insist that a daughter—rebellious or not—actively plot to destroy her father. How far away from Dominic d'Tierrza was that, really?

The fact that he didn't have an answer for the question didn't sit well with him.

Nor had it settled any better later, after he'd shut down Yancy Grove and led her back to the dock.

He boarded the *Ibrahim* behind her and prepared for the journey. He showed her her accommodations, and this time, she took him up on the offer, pleading tiredness.

He didn't comment that she had woken from her nap more vibrant and bright than he'd ever seen her. There was no need to call her out on it when he was the one she was running away from. Besides, as glorious as her moonglow remained, her light had begun to fade. Faint circles edged her eyes and her shoulders slumped as she'd thanked him for the room and closed the door.

It would take approximately twelve hours to return to Cyrano from Yancy Grove. They had plenty of fuel and ample supplies—he believed in being prepared, though he had not planned to return to Cyrano so soon. Strange, how he had not set foot on the island in over thirty years and now was readying to return for the second time in less than thirty-six hours.

His last trip had had a very specific purpose and, by proxy, had an extremely firm time limit. This time he had neither constraint, and yet the journey was colored with an air of finality. His grand revenge, his life-long quest, his quest for the holy grail, had concluded, if not exactly to his specifications.

And what did he have to show for it?

Twelve hours of silent questioning and one more sunrise later, he spotted land. Having joined him at the helm, Helene watched quietly as Cyrano grew larger on the horizon.

When she spoke, the first time since he'd left her at her cabin door, she said, "So we're going through Andros?"

Something old and seismic shifted across his heart, a feeling so deep and timeless he could no more interpret it than shifting sands. He gave a brief nod. "We're going through Andros."

Muffling the motor, they stealthily approached Andros's sleepy port.

Andros was too small to be bustling, but

was an important specialty port due to its deep waters. More charming than even Calla, Andros was like nowhere else on earth.

Drake steered them through the latticed network of limestone caves quietly, tucking into a shadowed cove with familiar ease. It was not the first time he'd returned to Andros since his family's exile.

Located on the rainy side of Cyrano, Andros grew lush forested hillsides and verdant farms. The western-most edge of Cyrano's "Great Green Spot," a phenomenal patch of agricultural territory responsible for growing the bulk of the food produced on the island, Andros was a small, productive duchy that generated dependable and respectable income, had little to no trouble and the happiest citizens in all of Cyrano…according to a popular magazine survey.

Helene had been its steward for the past two years, and in that time, he knew, she had dutifully cared for it.

But it was Drake's stolen home, the cozy hills welcoming him, speaking to him through his blood and bones, rather than his head and eyes.

Leading Helene along a narrow path toward the main residence, he ran through his plan. It was basic and would see to her safe return, without putting him in the uncomfortable position of having to explain things to the authorities.

He trusted her, as foolish and novel as the experience was, to keep her word, and more, to stand by him should he face legal action. In a matter of days, she had swept in like a hurricane, devastating thirty years of planning in one fell swoop, and yet he could not hold it against her.

He had set out to seduce her, but he feared, in the end, she might have seduced him.

The path he took them on led to a hidden doorway built inexplicably into the hillside. He reached for the handle as if he had every expectation that it would be open, and it did.

Inside was a dark corridor, lit with flickering exposed light bulbs.

Confident in the confirmation of his memory, he led them down the corridor, around a corner and up a small darkened stairway that led to another door.

This door was locked. Drake pulled out a key, the action practiced, and the door opened into a completely innocuous storage closet.

Behind him, Helene's voice was filled with wonder. "It's some kind of smuggler's tunnel."

Drake shot a grin at her. "Exactly. It was built during the war of the city-states of the midcentury." The intimate pride in his voice was undisguisable. Like Calla, Andros was his home. But Andros was also more than that—it was his birthright, his childhood kingdom.

That he'd been forced away from it because of her father was a knife in the chest that never stopped throbbing. Or hadn't, at least, until he'd swooped in and stolen Helene d'Tierrza into his life.

He should be the current Duke of Andros. He had created in Calla what he missed so sorely, and yet leading them through staff corridors, deftly avoiding being seen, he could not deny it was still a mere facsimile of the home he craved. Like Yancy Grove, Calla was a lovely getaway. Andros was home, the place he was most at ease, even when surrounded by enemies with his plans in tatters.

They came to another doorway—this one he listened at first.

After seconds stretched into minutes of taut silence, his ear glued to the doorframe, he held two fingers up to signal quiet, then retrieved the same key he'd used on the earlier door.

As before, it worked easily. Drake stepped through, followed by Helene.

They stood in another quiet room, a pantry, though it was obvious from the lack of dust and tidily stacked dry goods that this room was in regular use.

"Through that door is the kitchen. The day staff will be in there. They'll be able to make arrangements to get you back to the capital."

She nodded, looking up at him, her eyes full of things she had to say.

She opened her mouth, then closed it and shook her head, then opened it again. "I'm sorry," she said.

They weren't the words he wanted to hear. Though what he hoped she would say he had no idea. Pulling her into his arms, he rested his nose on the top of her hair and drew in a long inhale. Then he tilted her chin, angling her face toward his one last time. Running his thumbs below her eyes and along her cheekbones, he leaned closed, pressed his lips against hers and kissed her goodbye.

And then, without speaking, he turned and left. If he had stayed a moment longer, he wouldn't have been able to leave at all.

# CHAPTER NINE

A WEEK AND a half later, Hel was in the worst shape of her life.

Despite being in the comfort of her own bed, and the warm bosom of most of her dearest friends and family, she'd slept horribly and felt sicker and sicker with each passing day since leaving Drake in Andros.

Once she'd made herself known, it was a simple thing to get dropped off at a public location, from which point she called the palace first and her mother second. Everyone accepted her story of escaping her unknown kidnapper and returning—how could they not? She was Helene d'Tierrza, captain of the queen's guard, indefatigable and unbeatable.

And right now, she was a strange shade of grayish green. Strange, because she hadn't experienced a second of seasickness through her adventure with Drake, and yet was feeling all of its symptoms now.

She wondered if there was such a thing as land-sickness, and if so, if one could suddenly develop it after having spent a short time sampling the seafaring life.

Real or not, it certainly wasn't helping her track down what had happened with Moustafa.

All that she'd been able to discern was that her cousin, in a move that made absolutely no sense to her, had sent the queen to the summer palace and placed Jenna on a leave of absence the very same day Drake had abducted her.

Zayn had quickly followed behind Mina, traveling to the summer palace and conducting business from there through Hel's absence. Though he had personally called to tell her how glad he was to know she was safe, and they'd spoken at length about her supposed escape, she had not known at the time to speak to him about Moustafa.

Mina, too, between being at the mercy of Roz for wedding planning and being completely in the dark as to what had led Zayn to reprimand Jenna, had been unable to explain the situation.

Trying to untangle the mess with a hollowed-out and aching hole where her heart should have been, and a nagging and persistent sense of nausea, was presenting her with an entirely new kind of endurance training.

Thankfully, though she never would have imagined thinking this, Mina was gone. The fact that Hel was not on official duty was a shocking saving grace. Normally, her work energized her. It was the thing she lived for, but now, the thought of it made her stomach roll.

Being a guard had given her something real and lasting to do for the first time in her life, a sense of duty and responsibility that the charity rebellions of her youth had lacked—the sense of independent self she'd been so desperately seeking. It had shored up her wobbly, childish hope to undo the ill her father wrought in the world, and made it a full-fledged adult goal and given her the power to enact it.

And, for a short time after the nightmare of

her engagement, it had been the only reason she got out of bed and got dressed every day.

Becoming a guard and making a promise to protect those who needed it was the reason she didn't just let the Tierrza duchy fall into disrepair in order to tarnish her father's legacy. The neglect would have been satisfying, but that satisfaction would have come at the expense of her tenants and the people who depended on her.

Being a guard was the reason she had female friends. She and Moustafa had been partners for nearly seven years, graduating together from the royal security academy. They were an unlikely pairing—the priory girl and the rebel heiress. After her cousin, the king, Jenna Moustafa had quickly become Hel's second-best friend in the world.

And from the moment she had watched Dr. Mina Aldaba, now Queen Mina d'Argonia, proud and disheveled academic that she'd been, walk through the chapel doors to become queen not long ago, she'd known she'd gained her most important responsibility and another dear friend.

Knowing that Mina was safe under the protection of the specially trained summer-palace security unit was a deep relief.

Even if it left Hel with nothing but time on her hands and too much to think about, an upset stomach and no idea where her partner had gone.

Tracking down Moustafa was the obvious best choice of her options. But short of calling her family, which she was hesitant to do, she had exhausted her resources with no luck.

And knowing that her resources were… considerable, that pointed to Moustafa actually being with her family.

Hel felt like an idiot. If anything truly terrible had happened to Jenna, her family would have been hounding Hel's heels like Cerberus.

Jenna's family was large, ever-growing, it seemed, and deeply interconnected. They were absolutely wonderful, incredibly tight-knit, insatiably nosy and unparalleled at ferreting out information. Hel liked to tease that the terrier spirit was what made Moustafa such a good guard. It was also the reason Hel had avoided calling. It wasn't wise to call on the Moustafas with heavy secrets on your heart.

But now that the idea had occurred to her she was certain that was where Jenna would be. The Moustafas were members of a long-rooted religious minority in Cyrano. They believed in big families, which made living close in the capital a challenge. Jenna herself came from a farm on the outer edges of a suburb that bordered the city.

Satisfied with at least that one thing in her world, Hel rolled onto her stomach, hoping the pressure might ease the persistent nausea.

"Darling, are you all right? Liza said you weren't feeling well. And do you mind putting a shirt on?"

Hel's mother, Seraphina d'Tierrza, stood at the entryway of her quarters, wearing, notably, loungewear. Seraphina d'Tierrza did not wear loungewear. Her hair, also, was not as it usually was, perfectly coiffed without a strand out of place. Instead, it was tousled and pulled back into a messy French twist, strands falling loose around her face, which itself looked…tired, rather than its typical perfect polished pearlescent.

Sitting all the way up, and then regretting the motion, Hel sent her mother a weak smile. "Just a stomach bug," she said. "And what's the point?"

Seraphina eyed her for a moment, her deep blue gaze drifting down to her daughter's exposed breasts before traveling back up to her face. "Helene Cosima d'Tierrza. The point is that once a daughter has breasts, her mother doesn't want to see them. Now put this on. I want to talk to you." Mildly indignant, ever proper, and eternally loving, Hel's mother held out a hand that held a blue cotton T-shirt.

Hel pulled it over her head, unable to ignore the comfort of the soft, thin material, despite the fact that her skin had become so sensitive lately that she'd taken to going shirtless in her room just to ease the chafing.

Her mother knew her well, though.

The shirt was made from the softest cotton, had no tag, was lightweight and breathable. Everything she looked for in a T-shirt, and the only thing she could stand right now.

Joining her daughter on the bed, Seraphina pushed the bangs out of her eyes, tucking them behind her ear the same way she had since Hel had been a little girl and her hair much longer.

Searching her daughter's eyes with her own matching pair, Seraphina said, "Tell me your symptoms."

Hel shook off the concern. "I'm fine. Really. Just a bit off. I'll be right as rain in no time." She smiled the same smile—the one that said, "Don't worry, everything's fine, I'm strong"—that she'd been giving her mother since she was in elementary school.

This time, however, Seraphina wasn't to be put off. "Your symptoms," she repeated firmly.

Hel sighed before offering her mother a brisk rundown. "Primarily nausea, but also elevated temperature, sensitive skin, mild vertigo." She tried the smile again. "Just your garden-variety flu."

Her mother closed her eyes and took a breath, then opened them again. "Helene. You're pregnant."

Sapphire blue locked with sapphire blue, and Hel had the strangest sensation of panic rising in the back of her throat, slick and oily. She fought the nausea and shook her head. "No. No. That's not possible."

Seraphina nodded, her expression a strange blend of happiness and sadness. "I suspected it when you asked Liza to tone it down on air fresheners."

Still shaking her head, Hel said, "It can't be…"

Seraphina smiled, her expression turning soft and distant. "I was the same. Couldn't stand artificial scents and so, so sick. Everyone told me it was a sign you would be a girl."

Beneath her, the bed trembled. Until she realized it didn't. She was trembling, like a leaf in the wind.

She was pregnant.

If she'd broken her vow before, she'd eviscerated it now. The line would not end with her. A part of her wanted to laugh, and laugh, and laugh, and laugh, and not stop laughing until they took her away somewhere.

Pregnant and alone. Her father would have

hated that, so there was at least a small silver lining.

Sitting as near to her as she was, it was an easy thing for her mother to pull her into her arms as she asked quietly, "What happened, Helene?"

Hel realized what her mother thought and pulled quickly back to look her in the eyes. "Nothing like that," she said, palms waving. "Nothing like that," she repeated, looking away.

Her mother let out a long sigh, dread shedding from her shoulders, and Hel was grateful she could at least reassure her on that front.

"Are you sure you're right?" Hel asked. Obviously, the only way to be truly sure would be to take a test, but she trusted her mother.

Seraphina gestured toward her T-shirt-clad chest. "If I hadn't already suspected I would have after your exhibition."

And just like that, the bubble of horrified tension in her chest burst, and Hel surprised herself by laughing, but not the hysterical laughter that had threatened earlier. The laughter of release.

Her mother's subtle humor had always tickled her funny bone in a way nothing else could, and it felt good to laugh, especially in the face of having absolutely no idea what she was going to do, but knowing her mother would be there with her, every step of the way. There was a lot wrong with the world, but some things would always be right. And she would have Drake's baby, to raise and love, freely and openly, with a fireplace and not a whisper of murder or revenge.

"So…" Seraphina's words trailed off.

Helene looked up at her, head tilted.

Seraphina cleared her throat. "I know young people do things differently these days, but do you know who the father is?"

Hel's stomach sank, another wave of nausea choosing that moment to overtake her.

Drake.

He would want to know that his wildest dreams had come true after all.

For an instant, Hel was filled with the urge to protect him, to keep his name a secret and protect both him and her mother from the truth, because once she said his name, she would have to reveal the whole story to her mother.

But she couldn't hold it in.

"Drake Andros."

Once again, confusion flickered across Seraphina's expression. "What an odd coincidence," she said.

Hel shook her head. "Not a coincidence..." she said. And then she told her mother the whole story.

When she was done, her mother looked aghast, face tilted to the ground, shaking her head to herself with an unfamiliar, sad smile on her face. "I never thought I would see the day."

"What day?" Hel asked, sitting up. "The day your daughter came home unwed and pregnant?"

Her mother cast her a mischievous smile. "There was a time when *that* was my greatest fear," she said.

Hel rolled her eyes with a laugh. Her mother had never had anything to worry about and she'd known it, despite Helene's show for the public. They had always been close, and there wasn't anything Hel couldn't tell her mother. Which did not explain the persistent sense of dread that grew with each of her mother's words. They'd been a team so long that Hel knew when she was about to say something she didn't want to hear.

"No," Seraphina continued. "I never thought I'd see the day you fell in love. And with Drake Andros, no less."

For a moment, time stopped.

"What?" Hel repeated.

Her mother frowned, confusion darkening in her eyes. "You did say Drake Andros was the father, correct?"

Hel shook her head and said, "No. I mean yes. He is. But that's not what I meant. The other part. What'd you say?"

Understanding dawned on Seraphina's face and with it, the brittle casing hiding the truth inside of Helene cracked, breaking open at the painful compassion in her mother's expression.

Hel shook her head. "No."

"I'm afraid so, my darling."

"No," Hel said, as if repeating would make

her mother's words go away, rather than worming their way inside of her until they burrowed so deep, to deny them would be to deny herself.

"I think so, my dear."

It couldn't be. She couldn't be in love with a man who tried to dictate, manipulate and force her major life decisions—it didn't matter how kind or observant or compassionate he was. She couldn't be with a man who wasn't above simply taking what he wanted, who pushed until he got his way, no matter how generous or dedicated he was. She couldn't love a man that refused her because she wouldn't bow to his will.

She couldn't be in love with a man like her father. It all started with love. All the years of hurt and disappointment of trying to please and then trying to displease—it had all started because her mother had foolishly loved her father.

Hel refused that life for herself and her child. "No. I said no."

It was her mother's turn to shake her head. "Real love is not really a matter of choice, my sweet. At least that's what your aunt Barbara said," she added with a shrug.

But it was all far too serious to shrug.

Expression pained, Hel grabbed her shirt at her chest and twisted, as if the motion might make some difference against the growing pressure in her chest. "No. No. That's not for me."

Because if it was true, it would make her like her mother had been so long ago. It would make her blind and weak when she had worked what felt like her entire life to be strong.

A bittersweet smile flickered across her mother's face. "You don't have to take it. But I think you should."

"What?"

"Don't let your chance at love get away, Helene. Don't let you father take that from you, too."

"But…" Hel shook her head, unable to get the words out.

Her mother waited, patient and steady.

She looked away. "You loved him, and look what it did to us."

"Oh, Helene." Her mother's utterance of her name sat heavy between them, bearing the weight of a thousand feelings, most of them tangled and dark. Seraphina closed her eyes and took a shuddering breath. As she exhaled, tears slipped from between her eyelids.

She stayed like that, breathing, still though she shook, for a while before she spoke. "Oh, Helene. Helene. Helene. Helene. I should have told you. Oh, my sweet, I should have told you so long ago. When you were so little and would ask me so many questions, I couldn't bear to tell you the truth. And later, well, I guess there were no more questions. But no, my darling, I never loved your father. He slapped any delusions of that out of me that night so soon after our engagement."

Hel opened her mouth. "But you said…"

Seraphina gently pressed her fingers against her daughter's mouth. "I told my daughter a fairy tale to spare her a nightmare. I was infatuated with your father, the way young girls are wont to get, but that is a far cry from real love. What I sense you have with Drake."

Hel shook her head. "It's not possible."

"I'm afraid so, my greatest love. You wouldn't be having his baby if you didn't love him." Her mother patted her knee, a grin lightening her features. "You're not that kind of girl."

Hel snorted. "I'm no kind of girl."

Seraphina smiled, wide and soft. "There's my girl. And speaking of girls, I'm certain you're having one."

Hel brought a palm to rest lightly on her stomach, hoping to settle the disturbed butterflies that fluttered there. She was pregnant. That she had passed even an instant with that not being the foremost concern on her mind spoke volumes.

It suggested she loved him.

If that was the case, other things began to make sense: the precision with which her mind recorded every detail about him, the way her body was drawn to his, the way she'd run away from him.

Her heart rate picked up, sweat beading at her brow.

She had done everything in her power to ensure that she didn't end up like d'Tierrza women before her—just another entry in the annals of aristocratic girls played out as pawns to advance the aims of their grand families.

She had thought she'd been the rebel heiress, a duchess and the captain of the queen's guard, that she'd refused to marry so many times that no one would bother trying any longer. And that she'd taken a vow of chastity to give him his ultimate comeuppance, that she'd done it all to frustrate and thwart her father's will and desire at every turn, but that wasn't right. She'd done it all because he terrified her. He terrified her so much she'd done everything in her power and imagination to keep safe from him. She'd lived in the public eye, endeared herself to the most elite security force in the country, and guarded her heart, the most dangerous thing of all, ingeniously ensuring that she'd never fall for a man like her father.

"Helene? Are you all right, Helene?"

Hel stared into the face that was a sneak peek into her future. She was taller than her mother, but otherwise her spitting image.

"I love him," she said dumbly, as if, as with

her pregnancy, her mother could be the one to confirm for her.

Heart in her eyes, Seraphina opened her arms wide, and Hel fell into them, silent sobs raking her sinew-and-bone frame.

She loved him and it was too late. They'd already said their goodbyes in the dusty light of the pantry, the salt and pepper in his beard and hair layered wisdom and gravitas over his foundation of sheer male perfection, and she knew he'd thought through everything—word, deed and action—before making a move.

He was autocratic and driven, but he was still the best man she had ever met.

She had broken her vow for him, and he had broken her understanding of the limits of joy and love and pleasure in return. And so she'd pushed him away.

Her heart squeezed, but even with her mother, she didn't cry. D'Tierrzas didn't cry. According to her father, d'Tierrzas struck.

But she would not add insult to her open heart by allowing this moment to be the one that turned her into her father.

She was cut from a different kind of cloth. The kind attracted to hard men. It seemed she was more like her mother than she realized.

She was the kind of woman who loved hurt. Strange, how often the two feelings danced together within her, as if they were each other's favorite partners.

Love made her vulnerable.

She couldn't breathe.

And to top it all off, she was pregnant.

# CHAPTER TEN

SHE WAS AS beautiful asleep as she was awake, Drake noted, as he slipped into Helene's room long after she'd settled into the movement and breathing patterns of deep sleep.

She had been even more attractive in her street clothes earlier that day, all legs and platinum and blue, absolutely thirst-quenching when the only thing he wanted was a long drink of water.

That had been his first thought when she'd popped into view.

There was just something sexy about knowing all that dangerous and deadly power was wrapped up in something as innocuous as blue jeans and tennis shoes.

His second thought was that she was a liar. By omission, yes, but a liar nonetheless. But he'd already known that.

Now, looking at her, he thought she was a beautiful sleeping liar, clad only in a T-shirt.

He had trusted her and she had turned out to be as treacherous as her father had been.

Moving in silence, he traversed her room with ease. Taking in the design as he went, he scanned the space for whatever revelations it might have to share about the woman he couldn't stop thinking about.

It should have come as no surprise to him by this point, but her taste was exquisite.

As she did in everything, in her quarters the color she gravitated toward was blue.

Varying shades of the color could be found all around—pillows, throws, piping, art...and beneath that, crisp, clean white. The combination was as refreshing as a cool breeze, an elegant nod to the sea and the sky without an overt beach theme.

He had entered by climbing the trellis that framed the side of her balcony, then opening the French doors into her bedroom.

The trellis was a silly feature, obviously a security risk.

Inside the room, her large bed was tucked

into its own nook, ensconced, cozy and separate from the other areas.

The great room was dominated by a large blue braided area rug, which was circular, and, if he wasn't mistaken, homemade.

It blended seamlessly with the rest of the room. In fact, it seemed as if the rest of the suite had been designed around it. The incongruity of its quality, everyday cotton, when compared to the incredible sophistication of the rest of the room snagged his attention.

But he wasn't here to ponder braided rugs. He was here to kidnap the mother of his unborn child, who slept the peaceful sleep of the innocent in her bed alcove, her breathing deep and even.

The soundness of her sleep would have concerned him had it not been an expected and direct side effect of the reason he was here in the first place.

Helene was pregnant.

Walking away from her in Andros had been about as much as he'd been able to manage in the two and a half weeks since they'd parted. Instead of returning to Calla, he'd remained in Cyrano, first staying in Andros, until it became too far away and he returned to the private docking in Tierrza that he'd first used to present his wild scheme to Helene.

How incredible, that he'd achieved everything he'd set out to do—that that wild plan had come so powerfully into fruition. Like so many grand achievements, reaching it paled in comparison to the hope and expectation— it hadn't been enough. Arriving at its summit brought no satisfaction, merely the new vantage point from which to see the next, bigger, even more elusive goal. This time, it was her love.

He'd realized it while living out of the *Ibrahim*—he'd made an art out of keeping tabs on her. Observing her comings and goings, noting her pallor, her altered sleep patterns, her visit to the doctor in which she had walked in confidently and been led out of by the hand by her mother. The intensity of his focus, the need to drink her in every day. He wasn't done where Helene d'Tierrza was concerned—he'd never be done until he'd secured not just her body, but her heart.

Watching her as he had been had also made it clear that she was pregnant. That she hadn't told him—and wasn't planning on telling him, if her behavior had been any judge— was something he would bring up with her after they'd discussed other, more important matters.

Standing over her, moonlight streaming in through the windows that encircled the bed, it was all he could do to not throw her over his shoulder and haul her out of there like a caveman of old.

Sensing him, she shifted in her sleep, her body angling toward him, her lips parted, breath catching at the same time. In sleep, her full bottom lip quivered, coral temptation.

Still sleeping, her cheeks flushed, the softest pink, faded in the moonlight but still high and bright along the angled bone structure of her face, contributing to the overall effect of her glow, illuminating the space around them in what felt like holy light.

He wanted to shake his head free of the flowery thoughts—he had never been a man for poetry—but could not seem to staunch the flow, despite her secrets.

Leaning down, he caught her soft, sleeping lips with his own.

Her mouth was its own sweet homecoming, more and more addictively familiar with every taste.

Unsurprisingly, her bed was firm, the give going only skin-deep, but comfortable nonetheless, steady and secure and just soft enough to be welcoming.

She softened into him on a sleepy sigh, her arms coming around his neck, the silken length of her skin brushing along his as they went, charged beneath the surface like lightning coated in velvet.

Pulling back far enough, he looked into her remarkable eyes. She was awake, her stare as cool as deep and alert as a well, and full of welcome.

Trailing a line of kisses along her jawline, around her ear and down her neck, he laid his sensual trail from her face south, pressing his lips along her collarbone, before trailing down the valley of her chest, and farther still, until he reached his treasure.

She tasted like salt and summertime, and his mind overlaid the moment with memories of licking sweet melted juice off his fingertips beneath a hot sun, infusing her flavor with the rush of forgotten freedoms and untethered joy.

She had been his from the moment he'd seen her throw her champagne glass at her father's statue, and he was territorial—even if she didn't believe it was real. And he sensed that was true. That despite all they had been through together, despite the fact she carried his child, she expected to return to life as normal when all was said and done—another grand adventure over and gone.

Breaking apart, once again at his mercy, he proved yet again that she was wrong.

He would prove it to her as many times as it took, as many times as she had to shatter beneath his hands, his mouth, his body, in order for the idea to take root and sprout.

Still ruthless and restless, he made his way

back up to her mouth, possessing her once more, absorbing her lingering gasps in his kiss.

He was hungry for her, his body demanding satisfaction even as his eyes drank in the sight of her. It had been a matter of weeks and he felt as starved for her as if it had been years, and that was a power she had over him. A power he didn't want her to see in his eyes for fear of what she'd do with it.

When she opened her eyes, he was caught in their blue web.

"Where'd you come from?" she asked, voice thick.

Turning from her, taking in the room, anything but her, he said, "I never left."

She nodded. "And you've been tracking me?"

"Yes," he said. He saw no reason to deny it.

"You came in through the trellis?" she asked. He nodded.

Rubbing her neck, she yawned. "That's crazy. I never sleep that hard."

His narrowed eyes shot to her, but her own were closed as she stretched her neck. It would have been a good opportunity for her to tell him.

She didn't.

His stomach churned and he looked away again.

Following his gaze, unaware of his inner turbulence, a grin stretched across her face, her chin taking on the arrogant tilt he had learned to find both maddening and delightful, and she said, "That was my first win against my father."

He lifted an eyebrow at the rug. There were at least a hundred shades of blue in it, its huge round form taking up a remarkable amount of space.

She laughed, a little breathless in her pride, even now, what he imagined was a long time later.

"You made it?" he asked.

She nodded. "It took two hundred and sixty-eight T-shirts and an entire summer to secretly complete. I got the idea online and when I showed my parents, my father said, 'Playing with garbage is for trash, Helene.' Mother and I redesigned my entire suite around it."

It was a small battle, but he could tell it was meaningful. "How old were you?" he asked.

She looked out the window in an evasive move that was obvious. "Ten."

At his side, his fist clenched, though he had intended not to react. "A big project for someone so young."

She turned to him then, wearing a real smile, unguarded and true, as opposed to sarcastic and unbothered, and it hit him like a blow to the solar plexus. Resisting the urge to go to her, he frowned, but the expression did nothing to dim her light.

"My mother said something along those lines. She loved it," she said. Her voice always softened when she spoke about her mother. A phantom of sadness flashed across her clear blue eyes, but when she spoke, her words echoed his earlier thoughts. "I'm the only one who's ever been able to stand up to him."

He wondered if she realized how often she slipped into present tense when speaking about her father.

Haunting his daughter was just another sin to add to Dominic d'Tierrza's long list. Not for the first time since he'd learned of the man's death three years ago, Drake wished him back to life, just for the chance to be the one to destroy him. Now that his plan had been achieved, however, he would have to settle for stealing his legacy.

But not without settling things with his daughter first. She'd earned that much.

"It's no small feat."

He could see her blush, even through the darkness.

With forced lightness, she chuckled. "No one had ever accused me of having small feet."

Laughing softly, his voice playful in a way even those closest to him wouldn't recognize, he said, "Oh, really?"

"I bet you never thought death wore a size-eleven heel," she said.

He snorted. "My death doesn't wear heels at all. My death is a kindly elderly lady who prefers house slippers and nodding off peacefully in front of the television."

She laughed. "You're fooling yourself if you think that's true. You're a pirate, for crying out loud."

"Privateer," he corrected. "I have legal authority to take every prize I bring in."

She quirked an eyebrow. "*Every* prize?"

This time he laughed, perfectly picking up on her meaning. "Perhaps not *every* prize," he acknowledged. "But, one small deviation does not a pirate make one. I am a respected retired navy admiral. I have earned my rest and my peaceful passing. Unlike some of us, I'm content to go gently into that good night. I somehow get the impression you're more the down-in-a-fiery-blaze type."

Helene shook her head exaggeratedly. "Absolutely not. I'm more the disappear-in-a-transatlantic-flight type."

"Not you," he countered. "Too subtle. You're more direct than that."

"Speaking of direct… Why are you here?" she asked, bringing it all crashing back to reality.

He was here because she was carrying his child and keeping it from him. He was here not just to devour her, but to take her heart, as well.

"You're pregnant," he said. She wasn't the only one who could be direct. "What are the odds?"

The color drained from her face, the pallor quickly bolstered by her lip curled in disgust as knowing dawned on her face. "And you're here to collect for your revenge?"

He placed a finger on her lips, shaking his head with a smile. "No. You're pregnant, and I am in love with you. And I'm going to marry you, whether that means I have to accidentally kidnap you or not."

As it had the first time she'd gotten a look at him, her mouth dropped open, and while it wasn't words, he had to smile at the expression on her face, a wide grin stretching across his own. As it had that not-so-long-ago day, appreciation and hunger lit her eyes.

Today, though, she didn't run. Today, she sat up, leaned into him and gently laid her palms on either side of his face. She looked at him closely, as if memorizing his face, then took one long slow blink, opened her eyes and said, "I love you, Drake Andros."

Something shifted within him—was knocked over, cracked and grew bigger. And for the first time in his life, Drake Andros, the exiled duke, scrappy sailor, deadly admiral, vengeance reaper and feared privateer was satisfied.

Wrapping her in his arms, he held her with all the joy that sneaking into her room late at night prevented him for shouting.

And in the end, it turned out he didn't have to kidnap her.

When she finally stopped crying, and after she finished showing him exactly how much she meant it, she took his hand and followed him down the trellis.

# CHAPTER ELEVEN

SHE STILL COULDN'T believe they were getting married.

She'd slept for thirteen hours straight once they'd arrived in Calla and woken with a thirst unlike any she'd ever had before. Even the strange realities of pregnancy felt brighter, since she was facing the future with the man she loved at her side.

And now, she sat on her private balcony, situated off the suite, viewing the sea. The same staff person that had helped her before had delivered her wedding attire, which was lying out on the bed in the room behind her.

She was taking her mother's advice, and even Drake's—she wasn't giving her father another moment of her life. He was dead and she was going to live, not in penance for his sins, but because she deserved happiness after surviving him.

She and Drake did together.

As unorthodox as it was, he'd planned their entire elopement, down to ordering something special for her. She'd expected something ridiculous, only to be stunned by what she found.

Her bridal attire was made of exquisite, featherlight linen, comfortable and loose-fitted while remaining flattering. She'd appreciated the way the wide cut of the pants and the long brightly embroidered sleeveless tunic gave the illusion of added length to her already wiry frame. She loved the ensemble on sight, knowing it would look elegant on her without restricting her movement in the least. The cut emphasized how slim she was in the middle, and the assists she had, while the lovely embroidery, with various shades of blue, from cornflower to aqua to navy to sapphire, distracted from the fact that she had more hard angles than curves. And when she had seen herself in it in the mirror, she gasped, because, despite the fact that she had been draped in bespoke couture since before she could walk, it was the first time she'd ever worn something that had so obviously been selected with her in mind. Not her role, her utility, or her power—just her. Her personality, her thoughts and her needs. The flats that accompanied it, supple, flexible strappy things that moved with her feet, yet were delicate and pretty at the same time, were further evidence that the mind behind the ensemble had taken in every single detail about her since their meeting, observing and tending to her each and every need.

And it wasn't a dress.

In fact, her wedding was shaping up to be nothing like what she had imagined it would be. Granted, she had been six years old the last time she'd imagined her wedding, but even the rough outline she'd formed in early childhood had taken place in Cyrano surrounded by friends and family.

Instead, she was to meet her groom where he was waiting for her on a boardwalk by the sea in his lovely harbor city, their nuptials attended only by the officiant and the witness he'd brought to the island for the event. That nuptials were to occur at all, intimate and private or not, was truly a shift in fate.

But when she arrived, even that expectation turned out to be off.

Rather than the small group of strangers she'd expected, standing on the pier was her mother, as well as King Zayn and Queen Mina.

Tears glistened in her mother's eyes.

Zayn, as always, looked bored. "It took you long enough, cuz."

Hel opened her mouth to retort back, but before the words came out a pair of long, golden-brown arms pushed the king out of the way.

"I told you not to be antagonistic!" Irritation colored the woman's voice as the owner of the arms stepped aside to get a better look at her.

"Mina." Hel's sense of relief at seeing the queen, safe and sound, was smaller only than her joy and surprise at having one of her dearest friends, with her heart of a gold and brilliant mind to match, at her wedding.

Hel felt recharged merely standing in the warmth of her hazel gaze.

Crossing to her with long-legged strides, Mina drew Hel into a warm, summer-scented embrace.

Smiling her bright, far-too-open smile—the one Hel despaired of her ever learning to guard—Mina said, "I missed you."

"I missed you, too. A lot to catch up on."

Mina said dryly, "That's an understatement," and Hel laughed.

"We came here as soon as someone was sure it was safe for me to leave the summer palace." Mina rolled her eyes and thumbed in the direction of the king, but Hel was in agreement with Zayn. She wouldn't have approved of Mina remaining in the capital without both of her regular guards.

"Where's Moustafa?" Hel asked, noting her partner's absence.

Guilt dimmed Mina's smile, made it tight. "When it rains, it pours, eh? I'll catch you up on that, later. For now, we have more pressing matters. Namely—you getting married."

Instincts on alert, Hel wanted to know more

about Moustafa, but had a feeling that was a story she was going to have to wait on. Zayn and Drake eyed each other with barely restrained hostility, which she supposed had to do with a combination of the kidnapping and Zayn being the only living male relative she had remaining. Her cousin was nothing if not traditional.

After hugging her mother and once again exclaiming with Mina, the small group took their places. Hel's mother walked her down the aisle toward Drake, who, true to his word, looked for all the world like a man marrying the love of his life.

They said goodbye to everyone on the pier when Drake made the announcement that they would be taking their honeymoon at Yancy Grove.

What she thought was going to be a nightmare had turned out to be a dream.

Leading her down the docks, he took her not to the *Ibrahim*, but to yet another one of his personal fleet: the *Andros*.

The *Andros* looked like something out of a

top-secret operation: all black, opaque, sleek and sharp enough to cut a diamond, this boat was made for speed and sex.

They'd use it for both.

The cabin's wing door opened with his voice command, lifting out of the way for him to walk them down the steps into the spacious interior.

From the outside, the *Andros*'s antireflective exterior and aerodynamic design gave the impression of smallness, but it was a false one. Black was such a slimming color. The Andros was outfitted with a captain's suite, full gourmet kitchen, guest suite, lounge, library and sky-lit, central-navigation room.

He passed all of it without comment, intent on getting her into his bed.

As it always was, the energy between them was electric. Snapping and crackling, it was a constant reminder that he would never be able to contain her, that she was lightning, meant to strike.

If that had been her mission, she had accomplished it, achieving proximity to him he couldn't think of anyone else reaching on the eve of her disappearance.

He had taken her. She had taken his world by storm.

He would take her now, tonight, as many times as she could handle before they expired.

And it wouldn't be enough.

Fortunately, they had the rest of their lives.

Finally, after the eternity of time it had taken them to get there, he lay her on his bed.

Her eyes were the sea—blue, deep and greedy, sparkling and glittering as they caught every glimmer of the low light in the room. She was beautiful, ethereal and deadly, like an ocean creature—a thing of beauty and danger.

But she posed no more danger to him—the worst had happened. She had harpooned his heart and he was caught. Destined to bleed out when she removed her weapon, or be taken as her prize—doomed either way.

It was a sailor's fate to drown at sea, though, and if he was going to go, he vowed he would plumb her all of her depths before.

She was stunning in the clothing he'd had made for her. He watched her move with fluid ease, her attire attuned to her in form and function for the first time since he'd known her. She was fluid grace, her body in motion a thing of beauty, like a racing thoroughbred or foreign sports car.

Slipping an arm under her back, he lifted her mouth to his. She opened for him without resistance. Offering everything up for his plunder with a moan and he took it, before she had the chance to take it back.

Unzipping her tunic, he followed the line of her spine all the way down, curving his palm over the swell of her behind in one smooth motion before bringing his hand back out to slip the shirt over her shoulders.

Beneath the tunic, her moonstone skin glowed.

Her bra was blue, made of supple silk, and hand-sewn. He had not been an expert on ladies' underthings prior to outfitting her. He was now.

If it concerned her, it necessitated expertise. She lifted her hips so he could slide the trousers over and down her hips, freeing legs as long and lithe as a river snaking to the sea.

Her panties were lacy boy-shorts, with a tiny bow front and center, also blue.

Taking a moment to simply soak her in, he marveled at her pearlescent skin, silky smooth and clear as a cloudless night, and her slender, well-muscled limbs, each one honed and strong, an elegantly designed weapon at her disposal.

But nothing was so powerful as the mind and soul behind her appearance. The knotted net that had ensnared him. He'd realized it the moment he'd watched he walk away and realized nothing else mattered, not revenge, not justice, if she wasn't there to share his life. He was entirely at her mercy.

So he balanced the scales now by making her beg here.

Her panties followed the path of her trousers.

He brought his palm to her hip, driven with unexpected urgency and strength to run his hand down the incredible silken length of her thigh. Had he ever met a woman with softer skin? He couldn't recall.

It was as if every woman that he had ever known had disappeared from his consciousness, their memories cleaned and cleared from his mind in order to make room for her, for this.

She shared herself with him alone, it seemed only fair, he be born again, every woman created in her image. And though he'd sworn excruciating slowness, he could no longer resist the urge to taste. He covered one rose peak with his mouth and reveled in the sound of her moans echoing in the cabin.

Her legs were quivering before he moved to the other side with his attention, and, after only a few moments of attention, she was falling apart in a symphony of cries and gasps he felt as if they were his own.

Returning to earth and emboldened by pleasure, she met him with the fierce intensity she brought to everything, incorporating everything she'd learned from each of their previous kisses.

The effect was as powerful as a nor'easter,

enough to rip everything he'd ever known about the meeting of lips out by the roots and unmoor his understanding of the limits of human joining.

He shuddered, desperate to once again be inside of her, desire and need swirling, raising the inner alarm that he was entering dangerous territory, the space where implacable goals were set.

He wanted her in every way, all at once.

With a small shake of his head, he broke their kiss gently, drawing his focus back to pleasing her, noting how easily she tempted his control, her responses a siren call luring him to pillage and plunder when restraint was required.

Because for all her worldliness, the billionaire heiress and tabloid duke, eternal darling of the gossip rag, was still a relative innocent.

For a little while longer, at least.

He was a pirate, after all.

Sweet summer child that she was, she had so much to learn. His grin showed enough teeth to warn any girl that she might be dealing with a Big Bad Wolf, but she was too drunk on pleasure to take note. All the better to eat her.

She moaned and gasped in response, each sound punctuated by a small tremor, each one unique, never repeated and utterly intoxicating.

He was harder than he'd ever been in his life, and she had no idea of the sweet misery she was causing in him. She was lost in the storm, and just as he directed, mindless to his agony of wanting her.

And if it hurt, it felt that much sweeter to have her melting in his hands, this powerful woman completely his to do with what he wanted, an amazon, unconquerable but for him. He traced her soft outer lips, running his fingertips along her slightly parted, slick, opening with smooth caresses. She pressed her hips against his hand, instinctively grinding against him as he teased the sensitive bud at the top. He slid a long finger between her swollen lips and along the inner edges of her opening, and she cried out his name.

He let out a low growl, the sound rumbling

up from the place inside of him that knew he would never, ever let another even try for.

The thought became the voice inside demanding he claim her, make her his irrevocably. Her body trembled, the tremors racking through her telling him all he needed to know about how close she was the edge.

In truth, they had not even begun the feast there was to be had between their bodies. If anything, this sweet heaven—the melody of her moans, her taste electric on his tongue— was merely the first of a long train of delectable experiences that were to be experienced with her. And if he got too carried away with the images flashing through his mind, they were going to carry him away to bingeing rather than savoring. They would have time for all of it.

It was his pleasure to be both for her—the anchor that held her there, safe, protected, guided through unknown waters, as well as the gale force that swept her away, the hurricane that broke her apart and remade her.

But if he remade her, she, too, ripped him apart and put him back together as she wanted him—devoted and unable to ever deny her, he would spend the rest of his life reminding her of that fact.

Later, after they'd exhausted their bodies and he'd fed her and they'd sat together at the helm, beneath stars that were vast enough to swallow even the greatest distrust, companionable in a way he'd never experienced with anyone else, he looked into the eyes of the daughter of his greatest enemy and said the words he once had such a hard time admitting.

"I love you."

And the joy in her face was like the sunrise, though dawn was still hours away.

# EPILOGUE

IT HAD BEEN one month since Hel and Drake had relocated back to Cyrano. Nya had decided to remain in Calla, having spent most of her life in Sidra.

Tierrza was no more. As they'd plotted, Hel and Drake, with the help of the King and Queen of Cyrano, had unified their titles and lands under the name Andros and relocated the seat of the duchy to the port that Drake knew like the back of his hand.

With Hel on enforced maternity leave—enforced by Seraphina, Mina, Zayn and Drake—the queen had returned to the summer palace, temporarily relocating until her security situation was resolved. She insisted it was for the best, as it gave her and Roz the undisturbed time they needed to plan a wedding that was to go down in Cyrano's history books.

As Hel had suspected, when she finally tracked down Moustafa, she learned her friend had returned home to her family. It continued to be shockingly hard to gather details about what had happened with Jenna in her absence, but she and Drake would be making the trip out to the Moustafa farm to find out once and for all in a matter of days.

She had a great deal to catch up her partner on.

Prior to returning to the summer palace, the queen had made the suggestion to offer Drake a position in the national security council of Cyrano as a naval security adviser. Hel was ecstatic when Drake accepted the position, ensuring that, after the baby was born, she would indeed be able to return to her position as the captain of the royal queen's guard.

And for the first time since the event had begun, after sitting down together, Drake, Hel and Seraphina had decided to retire the annual Dominic d'Tierrza gala, conceiving of a new event and charity named the Ibra-him Andros Foundation.

Hand in hand with her husband, assured by her doctor that there was an end to morning sickness in sight, and free from her father's ghost for the first time since before he'd even died, Helene finally threw in the towel.

Together, they'd beaten him, and now they had the rest of their lives, free to enjoy, hap-pily ever after, together.

\* \* \* \* \*

# LET'S TALK
## Romance

For exclusive extracts, competitions and special offers, find us online:

- facebook.com/millsandboon
- @millsandboonuk
- @millsandboon

Or get in touch on 0844 844 1351*

For all the latest titles coming soon, visit millsandboon.co.uk/nextmonth